Code Name: Werewolf

'Wine Cellar' was hardly the description for the cave filled with row after row of enormous wooden casks. Two musclebound unfriendly types stepped out from behind elephantine casks to either side of me. In their hands they gripped broadswords as big as my arm.

I dove between two casks and crawled to the next aisle. A broadsword sliced down at my shoulder. Desperate, I made a run for the ramp leading to the vineyard and squirmed around the cask at the top.

Single file, they stalked up the ramp for the kill. I turned and slashed at the rope by my side. Their eyes grew large as the rope parted and the cask lurched off its blocks.

They tried running back down the ramp, but a 1,000-lb cask gathers speed awfully fast. The thugs disappeared underneath it, their anguished screams drowned by the flood of sherry which coursed over the stones from the broken cask. I dipped my finger into the sherry that hid the bodies, and tasted it.

Amontillado. Vintage 1968. A good year.

Code Name: Werewolf

Nick Carter

TANDEM
14 Gloucester Road, London SW7

Originally published in the United States by Universal-
Award House, Inc., 1973

Published by Universal-Tandem Publishing Co. Ltd, 1973

Copyright © 1973 by Universal-Award House, Inc.

Made and printed in Great Britain by
Hunt Barnard Printing Ltd., Aylesbury, Bucks.

Code Name: Werewolf

CHAPTER ONE

The bulls ran ahead of us, over the rolling Andalusian countryside. The sun was warm and brought out the gloss on their black hides. It brought out a thirst for sangría in us.

This was my vacation. Nick Carter and AXE were as far from my mind as Washington. For the time being I was Jack Finley, and I was nothing more romantic than an agent for an arms supplier. And Jack Finley was having a hell of a good time.

The Countess María de Ronda rode beside me on her white Arab stallion. I'd had no idea, when we met on the beach on the island of Ibiza, that María was a countess. As far as I was concerned, she was simply the sexiest female then on the Mediterranean. Her white bikini barely touched her lush, olive body. She had large, dark, Spanish eyes, long, black hair, and a bright, laughing smile. It wasn't until the next morning on Ibiza, after a night of lovemaking that had shown me the incredible passion behind the laugh, that a hotel manager woke us with a ringing phone, and I heard her called *contesa* for the first time.

There was no longer any mistaking that she was a countess. The bikini had been replaced by a sleek riding outfit of Moroccan leather, the raven hair tied in a bun under a wide-brimmed Sevillian hat, and in place of the laugh was an imperious smile. At twenty she was owner and ruler of the largest and most famous fighting-bull ranch in Spain.

This was testing time on the ranch—when the two-year-old bulls were given their first taste of the bullring. The ones who passed would live another two years before they became full-fledged monsters, ready for the ring. The ones who failed went to the slaughterhouse. Death with a butcher's bludgeon or death from an artist's sword—take your pick.

"You are sure you want to do a little fighting?" María asked me. "I don't want to see you killed on your vacation."

I noted how easily scorn could suddenly appear in her liquid eyes. The smile invited me to back out.

"I hate spectator sports," I replied.

"I know that already," she said deliciously. "Let's go."

I slapped my horse, and we picked up speed,

going from a canter to a gallop so that we could cut in front of the bulls. There were a dozen of us on horses, including a trio of matadors from Madrid, two picadors with their long, steel-pointed spears, and buyers and caballeros. We strung out in a circle. The young bulls grunted angrily and tossed their horns. They may have been only two-year-olds but each weighed about eight hundred pounds and carried saber-sharp horns that were six inches long.

The herd stopped on a butte as we circled around them. This was their territory, and for the first time in their lives they were being challenged. Their eyes rolled with hatred and confusion as the hooves of our horses picked up a ring of dust.

María stood in her stirrups and yelled to one of her men: "Cut out the one on the end. We test him first."

The man darted out of the ring to within ten feet of the end bull. At once the bull was after him.

The rider was an expert. The dagger horns jabbed at the flank of his horse, but he cut back and forth, always just out of reach, teasing, luring the bull farther and farther from the herd until animal and rider were on a flat plain a hundred yards away.

"They say that Cretan sailors were the first to introduce fighting bulls into Spain," María said. Her face was flushed with excitement as she watched the ballet of caballero and bull. "The

Cretans were bull leapers. It took a Spaniard to stand and kill or die."

The rider broke away from the bull, and one of the picadors approached it. He pointed his spear at the animal's head and yelled, "*Toro!* Ha, *toro!*"

"If he roars or paws the ground, it is a bad sign," María commented. "The brave bulls don't bluff."

This one did not bluff. It drove straight at the picador, its horns seeking out the horse's belly. But the spear dug into the muscles of its shoulders —steel ripping through flesh—as the picador leaned over and tortured it. The bull attacked again and again, ignoring the pain.

"*Basta!*" María yelled. "Enough, we have a *toro.*"

The riders clapped. The picador pulled the point of his spear out of the flesh and galloped away. One of the matadors was already off his horse and, carrying nothing more than his cape, approached the infuriated bull.

"To see whether the bull charges straight or has a hook. Everything is noted down," María explained, and sure enough, I saw one of her men jotting down every characteristic on a clipboard.

"A little black book," I said.

"Something like that," she answered.

With a sideways shuffle, the matador sidled close to the bull. He was not a short man, and the bull's eyes were level with his. María had previously told me that the biggest bulls were bred in Andalusia.

The matador shook the red cape. The bull ducked his horns and went after it, charging straight and true and leaving a smear of his blood across the man's shirt.

The bull turned and charged again. The matador handled it easily, letting the animal turn in wide circles.

"You see, Jack," María pointed out, "he plays it slowly so the bull won't turn too fast ... swing its testicles into a leg and hurt itself."

"It's a *toro* all right," the matador shouted as the bull charged past him for the last time.

Another bull was singled out of the herd. This one was even larger than the first, but when it hit the picador's spear, it roared and pulled away.

"A bad sign," one of the buyers commented.

A different matador approached the bull. The animal threw up dirt with its hooves and swung its horns. The matador stepped within a foot of the beast, trying to provoke a charge. The bull looked from the cape to the man, obviously making up its mind about which to gore.

"Be careful, Jaime. A cowardly bull is the worst kind," one of the other matadors called out.

What a Spaniard has in overabundance is pride. The matador moved closer to the lethal horns.

"Once in Madrid they put a fighting bull in with a tiger," María said. "When it was over, they had to bury four men and the tiger."

Nothing moves faster than a bull over a short distance, and the matador was an inch away from this bull when it charged. I was fifty feet away and I heard the shirt ripping apart. The front half of it fell over the man's belt, revealing the fresh scarlet line drawn over his ribs. His cape fell and he staggered back, the wind knocked out of him.

The only thing saving his life was the bull's own cowardice. That gave me time to charge my horse in between the bull and the matador and snatch the man up by his hand. When I let him go, he was out of danger and laughing and slapping my back.

"You ride well for an American," he said as he mopped the blood from his cut.

"*Buey, buey,*" the man who was taking notes yelled. "It's an ox. He goes to the butcher."

María rode near me. "Your turn, don Juan," she said as she threw a fighting cape over the horn of my saddle, "if you are as brave standing still as you are running."

"I'm best lying down."

"Tell the bull."

A package of black dynamite on the hoof darted out on the testing ground. Knots of curly hair grew in between the scimitar horns. The rider who had teased him out of the herd seemed glad to escape.

"We saved this one especially for you," one of the caballeros called out to me.

"Do I sense a practical joke here?" I asked María. "Do they want to show me up?"

"They know you sleep with the *contesa*," María answered evenly. "They want to know why I chose you. You can back out if you want to. Nobody expects a salesman to be a Manolete."

The bull charged the picador's spear. The metal sank into his flesh, but he kept on coming, jolting man and horse back step by step. I slipped off my horse and took the cape.

"Remember," María warned, "move the cape, not your legs. One must have courage and intelligence in front of the horns. Stand still and move the cape slowly—control the fear and you can control him."

I'd heard words too similar to those from Hawk too many times but never with regard to facing a beast bred a hundred years for killing. And I never expected to hear them from lips like María's.

"Tell me one thing, María. If by any chance this bull of yours does get me, does your thumb go up or down?"

"It depends on where he gets you."

I walked out to the plain. The picador rode off, and the bull's furious eyes swung toward me. I didn't want to try the matador's classic shuffle, and I didn't have to. The bull came right for me.

Then I knew why some experienced matadors suddenly break and run from the ring. The ground shook from the barreling charging bull. I locked my knees and spread the cape. As he lowered his horns, I saw the gore of his hump. I gave the cape one last, decisive shake, and the horns swerved toward it.

The young monster plunged through my clumsy pass, nearly pulling the cape from my hands. I set my feet again as he turned. This time I passed him on the left. In my ignorance, I didn't know that this was the more dangerous pass. His shoulder grazed my gut, rocking me and smearing me with blood. The powerful smell of his anger filled my nose.

"That's enough, Jack," María yelled.

But by now I felt the attraction of this deadly ballet—a man with a cape controlling, hypnotizing, a primal force. I steadied my legs and shouted at the bull: "Ha, *toro!*"

The beast had the taste of the kill in his mouth, too. I spun slowly around as he followed the cape, then led him away with a crude, high pass.

"There's a real man out there!" a caballero shouted.

There was a geometry to the ballet that fascinated me. The bull charged on a straight line, then moved into a circle that grew tighter and tighter as my passes became smoother and slower. The slower and tighter, the better our ballet. And the more dangerous.

The dowel supporting the cape snapped. I held the cloth with both hands, leading the bull until my shirt was striped a dozen times with his blood. Only he and I were real. All the rest—the riders and María—faded.

A horn ripped the cape in half. I tried to fight with what was left. On his next charge the horn caught my shirt. As cleanly as a razor, its tip parted the cloth. The side of the horn smashed me to my knees. By now even I knew my luck was running out. The bull certainly knew it.

As I staggered to my feet, he took me right between his horns. I cartwheeled over his back and landed drunkenly on my feet. The bull measured me for one last charge.

"Jack!"

I saw María's white Arab racing in from the side. The bull hesitated at the diversion. Then it charged. My hand grabbed María's thigh and I swung up behind her, lying flat over the rump of the stallion. The bull's horns just grazed my boots before I pulled myself all the way up and we escaped. The Arab's white flanks were smudged with red where I crouched.

As soon as we reached safety, María jumped off the horse. "Jaime! Bring me a new cape and a sword."

One of the men brought her the articles. The bull stood alone in the middle of the plain, victorious. María walked out to meet him. She was as skilled as a matador, but after a couple of passes, I saw that she was not intent on giving me a lesson. She was out to kill.

The bull was tired. He carried his horns lower now and his charges were shorter than they had been before. María took the sword from its cape. The blade was three feet long and curved downward at the tip. She shook her hair from her eyes as she sighted along the sword over the horns.

"*Toro*, come here," she ordered.

The bull came. Its horns dutifully followed the

cape as she passed it low to the ground. Her right hand, the one holding the sword, plunged over the bull's charging head. The sword sought out the picador wound and, with the momentum of the bull's charging body, sank in right to the hilt as she pivoted away.

The bull stopped moving. Its eyes were wide with astonishment. There was nothing left to charge, and the sword's hilt looked like nothing more than a bauble on the crimson hump of the animal's back. It started to move in a circle; then its hooves began to spread, and I saw its eyes film over with death before its body even hit the ground.

CHAPTER TWO

"You have no skill," one of the matadors told me over lunch back at the de Ronda house. "No skill but enough courage and intelligence. You could learn to fight bulls."

"Not like María. You're forgetting that she killed him."

María entered the vast living room. She had changed from the riding habit to modest white pants and sweater and she seemed no more murderous than a vestal virgin.

"But María has been fighting bulls since she could walk," the matador explained.

For dessert the house steward brought in fresh Valencia oranges. He peeled them in one long corkscrew of orange skin. While brandy was being served around the room, I asked María why she had killed the bull.

"Because I was a little bit angry at it."

"Wasn't it a little bit expensive for you?"

"I have a thousand bulls."

"And these were not her very best, either," one of the buyers added.

"The ones with the oldest, truest bloodline carry a special brand," María agreed.

"And a special price," the buyer winced.

The Spanish midday meal is the big one. After it comes the siesta, a civilized practice that, unfortunately, has never spread to New York. We all dispersed to our bedrooms, in my case a room the size of a banquet hall, with crossed swords and tapestries on the walls and a great four-poster bed. I undressed and lit a cigarette and waited. Sure enough, in ten minutes María came in.

"You're crazy," she said.

She was still wearing her pants and sweater but as she pulled off the top, I saw that she was wearing nothing under it. Her breasts were amazingly firm, their tips bright pink and hard. She stepped out of her pants. The light from the window, diffused by maroon drapes, spread over the olive gloss of her thighs and vanished in the black triangle I now knew so well.

"Anyone who fights a bull must be crazy, especially a woman."

"Shhh."

She climbed into the four-poster with me. At once her hand went between my legs. We kissed and she slid a leg over me.

"You are ready, aren't you?" I whispered in her ear.

Her fingers tangled in my hair as I rose up in her as smoothly as the sword had slid into the bull. We rolled over and her legs locked around my back.

María held on to me as though she were dying, yet she was never more alive. There was nothing of the aristocrat about her now. She was basic female, demanding and intimate, her lips seeking out my tongue as her hips embraced me in a velvet grip. The four-poster's canopy rocked overhead, slowly at first but with building speed.

Her black hair covered the silk pillow, and her eyes were wet with urgency. The bed trembled as we exploded as one.

Some men feel sad after sex. I never do. I would trade scotch, LSD, marijuana, and every medal they ever tried to give me—simply for that after-lovemaking buzz. I cradled María's head on my shoulder while her fingertips roamed my chest.

"You have too many scars for a salesman, Jack," she said dreamily.

"You have too much sex for a countess. We're even."

We went to sleep with her lips pressed against my chest.

We woke up thirty minutes later, when one of the servants knocked on the door. "There is a phone call for you, señor Finley."

María hid under the sheets as I slipped out the door. I became angrier with every step. Only one person knew where I was. I stuffed my shirt inside my belt and took the call on the phone at the foot of the stairs.

"I hope I'm not interrupting anything," a flat, nasal voice said.

It was Hawk.

"You said 'bon voyage' when I left. You don't have to say it again." As if that would be what he was calling about.

"Ah, well, I'm afraid that's not why I called. I know how you deserve a vacation after the episode in Chile," he pretended to mourn. Hawk's idea of a vacation is a sunlamp over the confidential files. "But something has come up."

"No."

"Business, N3." The humor was gone from his voice. Another clue to his seriousness was the sudden use of my rank in the organization. "An extremely sensitive transaction that I can trust only to you to carry out. I regret the inconvenience, but duty calls. Be ready to leave in forty minutes."

Hawk knew his man. At that moment I stopped existing as Jack Finley and became Killmaster, a transformation that I made reluctantly but instantaneously.

"A big sale?" I asked.

"One of the biggest. Pure TNT."

María was still in bed when I returned. Her black hair spread over the pillow, her breasts had the flush of renewed excitement, and the sheet clung to the curve of her hip. Somehow I managed to pack my bag.

"You're leaving?"

"Not for long, María. A little transaction."

I stepped into the bathroom to strap the shoulder holster inside my jacket and fasten the stiletto inside the cuff of my left forearm. At the hollow of my ankle I taped the slim gas bomb the Special Effects Department had designed for me. When I left the bathroom, I was Number Three, the top agent of AXE, Washington's most hush-hush organization. But I envied the arms salesman I'd been a minute before—he would have been back in bed with María.

Hawk was efficient. There was a car waiting for me by the time I'd given the countess a farewell kiss and gone downstairs. I got in and we drove off toward the town of Ronda, but halfway there the driver turned off toward the coast. On a promontory overlooking the Mediterranean we met a helicopter, and I switched to that.

The chopper lifted up and backed away from the cliff. I could see fishing boats drifting below us. My pilot looked at me for the first time.

"I could have sworn you were Henry Kissinger," he told me.

"Do I look like Kissinger?"

"Not much. But the United States Navy won't lend an unmarked helicopter to many people, mister."

We flew to zero altitude, cutting close to white-washed houses and flocks of sheep that grazed on the oceanside cliffs. Vacationers waved at us from the beach.

"Why are we avoiding Spanish radar?" I asked. That was the only reason I could figure that we were flying so low—not because the pilot wanted to scare some sheep or see bathing beauties.

"Brother, that's what I'd like to know. All I know is that my orders are to mow the grass."

We were flying west. As we drew near the buildings of the city of Algeciras, the chopper suddenly swung south over the water. I watched our shadow trail after us over the waves a mere fifteen feet below. Sea gulls exploded from the water as we passed by.

"Anyway, you can see where we're going now," the pilot remarked.

I couldn't miss it. The familiar insurance company symbol, the Rock of Gibraltar, loomed ahead. I could also understand now why we were chopping waves. The Rock itself is not actually an island but is situated on a promontory projecting from the Spanish coast. The Spanish want the territory back and the English won't give it to them. From time to time the Spanish try to starve the British out and the Spanish are always very touchy about what happens on the Rock.

We swung around to the blind side of Gibraltar. Built into the limestone cliffs of the Rock are naval guns, and we could make out the shadows of the gun bays. On our left was the African coast, a tan strip where the Mediterranean ended. Gamboling over the gun bays are the legendary apes of Gibraltar. The story is that as long as the apes continue to frolic, the British hold the Rock, and as long as they hold the Rock, the British control access to a sea that has witnessed more battles than any other on earth.

"Identify yourselves," the copter radio demanded.

"Seaview Tours," the pilot answered, although I didn't know of any tour copters that would weave through the radio masts of destroyers and cruisers the way we did when we approached the copter pad on the dock. I jumped down on the planks and almost landed on top of the United States Navy captain saluting me. I have an admiral's rating simply for priority purposes, and I suppose that Hawk had used it to get access to the British Navy's pad.

There were a few English naval officers standing around and an assortment of English and American Marines carrying submachine guns. There were also barricades with signs that said: "CAUTION—RADIOACTIVE AREA." Hawk had said the "sale" was TNT. It smelled more like an atom bomb.

Everything was gray paint, snappy salutes, and the creaking of chains as the ships lolled at the docks.

"Some vacation," I said.

The United States Navy, personified by the spit-and-polish commander, raised its eyebrows.

"This way, sir."

He led me to a covered pen the size of a football field. Once inside, the sunlight was gone, exchanged for the artificial glare of arc lights. Marines on catwalks patrolled with submachine guns. A bright-eyed ensign slapped a tag on my lapel. I'd seen that kind of tag before. If the plastic in the middle of it changes color from blue to red, you're "hot"—radioactive. This is supposed to be reassuring.

In the water of the pen were the ominous whales of thermonuclear war, giant submarines containing reactor engines and enough space for twelve intercontinental ballistic missiles tipped with hydrogen warheads. No doubt the missiles were Poseidons—bigger than the Polaris missiles and carrying three-megaton warheads. If anything ever hit the sub pen, Gibraltar would land on the moon.

"Please," the commander ushered me along the gangway toward one of the subs as though he were allowing me to go first in a supermarket check-out line.

I entered the A-sub's low, gray superstructure and climbed down into its claustrophobic bridge. Forget those World War II movies about sub-command posts looking like boiler rooms. This one contains one of the world's most compact computer centers. Little lights danced over control panels that read off, even while in dock, reports from radar and sonar, from the Rota Naval Command's NATO code center, from sensors on the sub's hull and sensors within the pulsing heart of its portable reactor, and most important, reports on the war readiness of its multitude of missiles.

"To the bow, sir," my personal commander said.

We pushed forward through a narrow hall. One thing about atomic subs is that they're roomier than conventional subs, and you don't have to squat when you want to take two steps. Once again we started running into signs stenciled in red paint that read: "RADIOACTIVE AREA, AUTHORIZED PERSONNEL ONLY." At the last door the commander spun the lock open, and I stepped alone into the missile bay.

Only I wasn't alone. One whiff of foul cigar fumes told me who was waiting.

"Isn't this supposed to be a non-smoking zone?" I asked.

From behind the first tube appeared Hawk himself. He's a small, thin man with an unerasable, sardonic grin and a wardrobe of interchangeable tweed jackets. Only a few men in Washington, London, Paris, Moscow, and Peking know about this man, a man so powerful he can commandeer a sub for a private chat. Hawk held his burning cigar without shame.

"Don't be bitter," he said. "I really do apologize for breaking up your vacation."

"Said the crocodile before he swallowed."

"Ha!" Hawk had a laugh like a backfire. "And I thought you'd be flattered that I came all this distance to see you."

I leaned against one of the missile tubes and

took one of my cigarettes out of a gold case, mainly to counter the stench of his stogie.

"Well, I am a tiny bit curious about the reason and also about why we're meeting here when the United States Navy has its own base at Rota, down the Spanish coast. It means that whatever it is, it's big and that our own security has been compromised."

"Precisely. Bigger than the missile in that tube if my suspicions are right, Nick, and even more delicate."

Hawk sat on a box beside a panel with two keyholes and the notation, "VOTE HERE." Votes mean the pair of keys that would have to be inserted by two different officers and turned at the same time to arm the missiles' warheads. From his jacket he took a water-stained leather envelope and handed it to me.

I removed a sheaf of papers from the envelope and scanned them. Plainly, they'd been submerged in water for some time, but a laboratory had reconstructed most of the missing words.

". . . depends on the liquidation of F . . . Werewolf received first payment . . . more money on execution . . . cooperation . . . no reason for doubt —Werewolf . . . successful in all other assassinations—of El R., in Yemen, Col. P., in Nicaragua and H. in Malaysia . . . no one to know identity before or after completion of mission. Now F. must die. F. is a traitor to his own cause . . . traitor F. must die. . . ."

The rest of the document went on in the same vein about the anonymous F.

"It certainly sounds as if someone has a contract on his head," I said as I returned the envelope.

"What else?" Hawk asked. His eyes glowed the way they do only when AXE finds a problem worthy of its best efforts.

"A professional assassin from the sound of it. Operating as a lone wolf. The letter is in Spanish, and there's mention of a general staff, which implies the Spanish General Staff in Madrid and explains why we're meeting here instead of Rota. The question is, who is this F.?"

"Just a little jigsaw, isn't it?" Hawk agreed. "The British took this from a man who died in the crash of a small plane near the Rock a month ago. Then the Russian fleet entered the Mediterranean last month, and while the Limeys were trying to intercept Red radio messages, they ran into another shortwave communication. I don't have any papers to show you but the transmission is short, and I memorized it yesterday in Washington. 'Werewolf arrived. Completion of mission promised by end of month. Plans ready for control of T.A.B., Z.A.B., M.A.B., R.N.B., C.Z.P. The call to arms is ready to be raised. F. must die.'"

For the first time the chill of the water traveled through the hull of the sub and into my blood.

"They're out to kill Franco," I heard myself say. "A professional killer has been hired to kill Generalísimo Franco."

29

CHAPTER THREE

"Only the chief of the Spanish Intelligence knows about the plot. He tried to tell Franco about it, but the Generalísimo won't take any extra precautions." Hawk shook his head sadly.

I could see why. Francisco Franco, Generalísimo, *El Caudillo* (The Warleader), had ruled Spain with an iron hand for nearly forty years. Just one of half a dozen Fascist rulers at the start, he had outfoxed and outlived Hitler, Mussolini, and Tojo—and made his dictatorship an indispensable keystone of NATO's defenses. He wasn't the prettiest ally we ever had—a crochety old man with a chest covered with medals he'd awarded himself and prisons full of Spaniards with a taste for liberty—but he had nearly attained immortality, and how many Fascists can you say that about?

"We know Franco can't last forever, and the United States is putting pressure on Madrid to come up with a more democratic form of government when he dies," Hawk continued. "But if Franco is assassinated, all bets are off. There are a dozen secret societies in the government, some monarchist and some so Fascist they'd give Hitler the bends. There's nothing I'd rather do than just let the Spanish settle this in their own way, but do you know our stake in this country?"

Indeed I did.

"Three hundred million dollars' rent for the land for our bases. Four hundred million spent building the bases. Billions in planes, ships, and communications centers."

That's when the light went on in my head.

"My God, those initials. T.A.B. That would be the Torrejón Air Base, outside Madrid. The others would be," and my brain was really rattling now, "the Zaragoza Air Base, the Morón Base, the Rota Naval Base. C.Z.P. is the Cadiz to Zaragoza pipeline. If we lost those, that would pop the whole NATO balloon."

"Now do you see why I pulled you out of the countess' bed?"

"But, but," I rolled my cigarette over my fingers, "the operation depends on killing Franco. They said so themselves. There must have been a hundred attempts on Franco's life—maybe twenty plots as advanced as this—and Franco's still alive. The Spanish may not have the best intelligence network around, but they've got a hell of a police force. They ought to, it's a police state."

"This time it's different. The Spanish secret police, their Guardia Civil, and the army M.I. are all designed to stop political agents," Hawk pointed out. "Sure, they've killed Loyalist agents trying to even the score of the Civil War and student Communists and Royalist plotters. They're good at that because they've always been good at infiltrating political organizations. This time they're up against a cool professional assassin for hire. Someone who operates outside of political circles, who can't be given away. AXE doesn't know Werewolf's identity yet, but we've been checking his record. There was a Sheik El Radmub thrown off a cliff in Yemen four years ago. As a result, his brother became ruler of an emirate floating on oil. Colonel Perugina blew up in his car in Argentina two years ago. Until then Perugina had been busy jailing labor leaders. Nobody dared do that after he died. And a Chinese politician, Ho Ping, just vanished in Malaysia last year after he double-crossed Peking on an opium deal. No cases solved, and each man was protected by armed guards. Whoever Werewolf is, he's the best. Except for you, Nick."

"Besides the flattery, what are you getting at?" Hawk rapped on the missile tube.

"This baby has multiple warheads because it has to overcome radar. The Werewolf is more efficient. No radar has ever picked him up. There's only one way to stop him. Match him with another lone wolf. You. Franco is well protected, but there must be a chink in the armor somewhere. Werewolf has found it, or he wouldn't have promised success so soon. Your assignment is to find that chink and kill Werewolf."

"With no cooperation from Franco or his bodyguard?"

"That's right. There must be some plotters close to the Generalísimo. They won't be able to tell you where Werewolf is, but they can tip off the organization about you."

I let out a long cloud of blue smoke. "A needle in a Spanish haystack."

"A gun in a Spanish haystack," Hawk grinned sardonically. "But I do have one more clue for you. There was no identification except this on the dead man who was carrying the envelope."

I looked at a stained business card, embossed with what might have first appeared to be no more than two lightning bolts, except that I recognized them as ancient Teutonic runes of the SS, otherwise known as the Schutzstaffel, Hitler's killer elite.

CHAPTER FOUR

Spain is a paradise for secret societies. Even in Franco's cabinet there's the powerful Opus Dei, a Catholic force of technocrats. Franco also has to deal with the Falange, the old Fascist society, and two different Royalist groups. Add to them the bitter French expatriate soldiers of the O.A.S., who nearly succeeded in killing DeGaulle, and then blend in a heady pinch of unreconstructed Nazis who escaped the war-crimes trials to become a prime business force in Madrid.

Where does the Werewolf figure in this? I asked myself as I flew on Iberia to Madrid. I had one ominous hint. I knew that when Nazi Germany was collapsing at the end of the war, the SS broke up into assassination teams, and each member of a team was known as a werewolf.

From the airport I took a cab to a dentist's office off the Puerta del Sol, in the middle of Madrid. The waiting room was full of suffering patients and limp rubber trees. In general, Spanish dentists are better with a pair of pliers than with a drill, but despite the gauze I'd wrapped around my face, I hadn't come to have my jaw excavated.

"Doctor Sereno will see you at once," the receptionist told me.

The other patients gave me the kind of relieved grins you'll find only on the faces of people reprieved for a few more seconds from a Spanish dentist.

"*Buenos días*, take a seat, please," Doctor Sereno said while he washed the blood of his last patient from his hands.

I slipped into the reclining chair and stared up at the dental lamp. Doctor Sereno dried his hands and approached the chair greedily.

"You know, your Spanish is lousy, Doc."

Doctor Thompson of AXE Special Effects, alias Doctor Sereno, cracked one of his rare smiles.

"I just hope I haven't pulled any wrong teeth today."

"Look, this is the one place in the world where no one would notice."

Thompson took the rag from my face and threw it into a wastebasket. He was in his element now, and that element was not dentistry. He opened up a small attaché case on the dental tray. Lying in velvet-lined compartments were spare ears, chins, cheekbones and noses, all constructed in the Special Effects laboratory, and each stained to the exact coloration and texture of my skin.

"This is something new I've worked up for you, N3," he said with professional joy. "No more polyvinyl chloride parts. These are made with siloxane, the newest plastic from NASA."

"NASA? I'm going to the royal palace, not Mars."

"Well, siloxane was developed to protect spacecraft from meteorites. Maybe it'll stop bullets, too."

"You know, you've got a hell of a bedside manner, Doc."

"Shhh."

I was as silent as the sphinx while Thompson went to work. In the reflection of the lamp I watched him remold my face, accentuating ear lobes, sharpening the bridge of my nose, adding the hint of an epicanthic fold to my eyes and widening my jaw line. As a final touch, he fitted my eyes with contact lenses that turned them Spanish black.

The trick with disguises is to avoid the major change. Beards, for instance, went out with Mata Hari. The more subtle the transformation, the more convincing, and I was going to have to convince some very tough customers.

"Fingers?"

I spread my hands, palms up. Thompson laid transparent patches of pliable silicone over the tips, giving me a complete set of new fingerprints.

"Of course, if something did happen to you,

they'd really identify your body by the dental plates," he remarked. "But I'm not trained to work on your teeth."

"Thanks."

I left with the rag wrapped around my head again to hide the work of the good doctor.

There are two royal palaces. One is the Palacio Real, an imposing Renaissance structure that tourists can visit, near the center of Madrid. The second is outside the city. It's post-Renaissance— much less impressive—but it's where the power is. It's El Pardo, the residence of *El Caudillo* Francisco Franco, and his very choice of location outside the city limits of Madrid was designed to protect Franco from the citizens of his own capital. During the Civil War Madrid was not a Franco stronghold.

Dressed in the dark uniform of a Spanish Air Force captain, I arrived in a Spanish Air Force jeep at a roadblock a mile from El Pardo. The roadblock was manned by members of the Guardia Civil, distinctive in their tri-corner hats. They examined my papers and waved me on. As I left, I heard them radioing my approach. I was just within eyesight of El Pardo when I hit the second roadblock. This time my papers were scrutinized by steel-helmeted military police. While they phoned ahead, I glanced around at a tightening ring of wire fences that were patrolled by attack dogs and soldiers.

At the gate to the residence itself I had to enter a waiting room inside a concrete bunker. My fingerprints were taken and my new face photographed. Both prints and picture were taken in to the officer I said was expecting me.

Of course the officer was not expecting me, and he would spot me as a fake as soon as I entered the palace. The phone in the bunker rang.

"*El capitán está aquí. ¿Hay un error?*"

The guard watched me over the telephone mouthpiece. "*El capitán dice que usted no está esperado.*"

"*Solo sé que tengo mis ordenes,*" I answered, using the age-old alibi about following orders.

"*Vamos a ver,*" the man on the telephone commented. "*El computador debe saber.*"

Now I knew the reason for the runaround with the photo and the prints. There was a computer on the palace grounds that would check my physical characteristics with those of the officer I was impersonating. I sweated for half an hour until Doctor Thompson's work passed the test and I was told to continue to the palace proper.

A landscaped garden surrounded the three-story palace, which was in fact no more than a country villa. A massive facade drifted quickly into a colonnade with French doors. Peacocks strutted around beds of flowers, and guards stayed within the shadows of the trees so that no unpleasant glimpse of them would ever be suffered by *El Caudillo* inside. Halfway along the walk a gruff muscular veteran of the Spanish Foreign Legion joined me without a word. I remembered that Franco had become the youngest brigadier general in the world when he was leading the Foreign Legion against Berbers in the Spanish Sahara before the war. This veteran wore a neat tan kepi and some lovely white scars. He was one of Franco's personal, devoted bodyguards, and any assassin would have to step over this one's body.

More Foreign Legion kepis appeared as soon as we were inside. I noticed a metal detector at my side, but I'd taken the precaution to come unarmed. Rightly so, because a second later I was shoved into a small room and thoroughly frisked.

"Your superior officer will come to get you," Scarface told me. His hand rested on the butt of a Luger that was a lot like my own.

I rubbed my eyes.

"What's the matter?" he asked, alert for nervous sweat.

"Nothing."

Hushed footsteps went past the hall on thick red carpets. I'd seen enough of the hall when I entered to know that the mirrors were one-way and that every visitor had a gun pointed at him every instant. No crown jewels were ever guarded like *El Caudillo*.

"You look sick," Scarface noted with growing interest.

"A little something I picked up in Angola," I passed off the beads of sweat on my cheeks. "I was observing the Portuguese bombing raids on African guerrillas. It will go away in a second."

39

"You're sick?" Scarface nearly lifted me off the floor by my collar. "You're sick and you dare to come to the palace? Idiot! Didn't they tell you no one is ever allowed near the Generalísimo if he is sick?"

He was tempted to shoot me on the spot. Instead, he hustled me outside. "I have been with the Generalísimo for forty years. I have killed a dozen men who dared to raise their voices let alone a gun, near him. I will kill you unless you get into your jeep and go."

"But I have orders."

He snapped the gun out of its holster and shoved it in my gut. "I don't care if they are from the Pope, señor. If you don't go now, you are a dead man."

I looked properly frightened and hightailed it back to my vehicle. As a matter of fact, I had heard something about the fear that visitors might carry infection to the aging Franco. You might even say that all the tea in Madame Mao's China couldn't have lured me into El Pardo unless I was sure that a sudden attack of malaria would get me out.

So much for scouting the lay of the land. Nobody was going to kill our esteemed ally during the day, so after ditching jeep and disguise, I returned at night.

In one way, I had an advantage. The Werewolf was working alone, without assistance of any kind. I could easily appreciate that. There's no one you can depend on like yourself. But it also meant that I could imitate his plan to the letter —without worrying about any of Franco's bodyguards providing the assassin with assistance I wouldn't be able to have. Whatever he could do, I could do. At least, that was the premise.

As soon as dark fell, I launched my attack on El Pardo. I was no longer Nick Carter, AXE killmaster. I was the Werewolf. The Luger was strapped over my pullover. Knife and gas bomb were in place. There's no simulation like the real thing.

The palace was ringed with three separate wire fences—I knew that from my drive in during the day. In the movies all the heroes cut through fences, which is why so few actors become good espionage agents. I did what the Werewolf or any good professional would have done—entered by the most guarded entrance, passing through the roadblocks themselves.

I waited by the first barricade until a jeep approached and was halted by the soldiers. Its headlights remained on, effectively dulling the soldiers' eyes to what passed in the dark on the side of the road. I could have strolled through.

I floated through in the shadows, past the second roadblock as well, but the third one at the palace gate was a different matter. Floodlights picked out every blade of grass. From the bunker there pointed the snout of a heavy machine gun. On my stomach, I eased over to the fence. Tendrils of grass grew in even rows. There were no dogs or soldiers.

It wasn't grass that was inside the fence. The whole inner ring around the palace was laid with sensors, grasslike antennae that quivered in the night breeze and sent back constant readings to Franco's computer. I recognized it only too well. The United States Defense Department had developed the eerie sensors to detect Viet Cong.

Through my sweater I felt the rhythmic whoosh of an engine. It didn't belong to a car. My head snapped up and I just barely caught sight of a black Huey Cobra helicopter hovering over the trees. It had a silent engine—something else developed in the United States—and if its job was surveillance, it had to have something else we'd created and handed over to Franco: ultra-violet heat sensors that would pinpoint me as neatly as if it were high noon. That plus its machine-guns and rockets.

The Cobra drew closer. Its scanners would already be picking up my temperature traces. On the screen I would grow in red hues from a rabbit to a dog to a man. I squirmed around on my stomach, thinking to retreat, but already a truck was approaching the gate and its headlights would only make the Cobra's job easier.

The truck was a hundred yards away, the gate thirty yards. The Cobra came to a halt in the air, its nose pointed straight down at me. The legionnaires at the gate answered a phone call and a second later a column of them streamed out of the bunker, running down the side of the road.

What would the Werewolf do?

I waited until the lights of the approaching truck picked up the Cobra, then I fired. The sensor pad exploded. I moved quickly forward, and the earth where I'd been lying was ripped up with fire spewing from the infuriated copter. I paused just long enough to shoot out the spotlights at the gates and then got to my feet and sprinted directly toward the legionnaires.

There were ten of them, all strung out across the road. With the lights behind them out and the headlights from the truck ahead in their eyes, they were partially blinded. I hit the one in front of me before he fired a shot, flying over him with one foot on his chest and the other in his face. As another legionnaire came out of the bunker, I chopped him across the throat, and he pitched to the ground.

A screaming peacock ran about, adding to the confusion. The copter was breathing down my neck again. More legionnaires spewed from the palace entrance and without even looking, laid down a field of submachinegun fire that cut down the peacock and a hundred flowers. I veered off to the colonnade of French doors. A legionnaire stood guard there. I tackled him, and we carried the glass door inside with us. I left him among the shards and ran through a ballroom. Harpsichords stood off to the side and massive crystal chandeliers hung from the ceiling.

A bulky figure blocked the exit of the ballroom. It was Scarface. I hit him with a dropkick that had about as much effect as a down pillow. He brushed my legs aside and seized my neck. The favorite form of execution in Spain is the slow, agonizing garrote, and he seemed to have a special liking for it.

Rather than fight his amazing strength, I ducked forward and threw the grizzled veteran over the polished dance floor. He laughed as he sprang to his feet.

"So we dance a little longer, friend, that's all," he said.

"You dance."

I moved behind an antique harpsichord and shoved it with every bit of muscle I had. It seemed to pick up momentum before it hit Scarface at the waist. He doubled over the keys and the two of them rolled over the dance floor into a door. Scarface crashed through it and landed in the garden. The harpsichord's legs gave out with the impact, and it collapsed to the floor with a concatenation of tinny notes.

I dashed down a hall. Franco wasn't supposed to know about my existence—but how could he possibly ignore the gunfire right outside his windows? And I had to know whether the Werewolf could successfully carry out his plans in the palace. I stripped off the shoulder holster and tucked it and my gun inside my sweater. Then, at the most massive door I knocked respectfully.

"Who is it?" an old man's voice asked with irritation. "What is all the firing about?"

"An accident, Generalísimo. Nothing more."

"Well, how can I sleep with this going on? These precautions can get out of hand," the voice said tremulously. "Tell them to stop the racket."

"I will, Generalísimo."

"Then go and do it."

Unfortunately, it wasn't that easy. There were twenty reinforcements waiting outside the front door.

I tossed the gas bomb in the center of the milling group and ran out through the smoke and gagging legionnaires, pausing just long enough to liberate a kepi. The truck that had followed me to the gate was parked beside it. I jumped in behind the wheel and started up without waiting for passengers.

At the middle roadblock I was waved through, but the legionnaires had gotten their message through by the time I reached the outer barricade. Guardia Civil motorcycles blocked the road and over the seats I saw tri-corner hats and submachineguns.

The cycles flew up in the air as I barreled through. The Guardia Civil was too busy rolling out of the way to do any more than put some holes in the back of the truck.

At the first side road I turned off and drove into the woods. There I donned the Air Force uniform and transferred to the jeep I'd cached after the daytime visit.

In that guise I joined the search for the mysterious assassin until morning and then I left for the

Palace. Only this time, the Palace was the most luxurious hotel in Madrid, and it has the kind of crisp sheets and soft pillows that let you sleep till noon.

CHAPTER FIVE

A witch, bearing her victim to a distant castle, flew through the air. A monster tore his children apart, eating them with savage bites. A coven of witches, goats, and devils met at night, their camp-fire casting eerie shadows in the gloom. All these beasts, and more, were gathered in one room of Madrid's fabulous art museum, each monstrosity a creation of the master painter Goya. Goya died of lead poisoning, a result of his incessant painting day and night with vats of lead paint. One of the symptoms of this disease is depression accompanied by foul nightmares. Now, a hundred years after his death, Goya's nightmares can still be shared by visitors to the museum. This was the place, surrounded by a madman's dreams, that Hawk had arranged for us to meet.

"You certainly did a job last night," he said

as if we were discussing some moot point of art history. "There are still roadblocks around the capital. I tell you to walk on cat's feet and you almost overthrow the country. Sloppy."

"But necessary. I had to know if the Werewolf could penetrate the palace guard."

He was angry but I could tell he was interested.

"And?"

"Yes."

A museum guard ushered in a tour. The guide leading it was a woman in tweed with heavily rouged cheeks. Her English was fruity and full of words like "soulful" and "cosmic sensitivity." Goya would have dumped her right in one of his vats of paint.

"Yes, but the Werewolf won't," I continued as Hawk and I strolled into the adjoining room. The first thing I saw there was Goya's famous *Naked Maja,* a voluptuous, dark-haired *contesa,* stretched out over a divan and gazing at the viewer with a come-hither smile. From an earlier period of Goya's life. At once my body was thinking about María de Ronda.

"You did," Hawk said, bringing me back to earth.

"And almost didn't get out. No, a professional like the Werewolf has to have a good escape route—he won't attack without one. Besides, after my visit security will be tighter than ever, and it was pretty tight last night."

48

"His accomplices might help him out after he carries out the assassination."

"True. But since they don't know who the Werewolf is, why wouldn't they have helped *me* out last night? Believe me, I got no help. Incidentally, I didn't kill anyone, did I?"

"No. But their infirmary has new business," Hawk answered tersely.

He may not have liked my methods, but I knew I had some good results. Now we could be sure that Franco's bodyguard was loyal and that Franco was safe as long as he stayed in El Pardo. What I had to admit was that I was no nearer to discovering the Werewolf. If there was a Werewolf, that is.

"It doesn't make sense," I muttered. "Just the name itself, Werewolf. That's a name a fanatic would use for himself. Professional killers aren't fanatics—they can't afford to be. He could be a fantasy just like these paintings. Secret societies live on fantasies. We could be chasing our tails for months because one crackpot wrote another."

"When you could be taking your vacation, instead?" Hawk glanced at the *Naked Maja* as he spoke.

It was no go. Hawk flew back to Washington in the afternoon, and I stayed behind to chase my phantom. Naturally, the first thing I did was call the hacienda of María de Ronda. I learned that she was in Madrid and—even nicer—when I called her Madrid number, she said she would drop everything to see me. "See me" was not the exact phrase she used, and I thought again of Goya's *Maja*.

We met that evening at an outdoor restaurant in the Plaza Mayor, one of the handsomest squares in Europe, and María was the loveliest female there. Again she was dressed in white, highlighting the olive tone of her skin.

"How did your sale go?" she asked as we shared a duck baked in Valencia oranges.

"A helicopter deal. Nothing exciting."

"Too bad. You haven't even heard the rumors. There was an assassination attempt on the *Caudillo* last night. Whoever it was just barged into the palace and escaped. He must be quite a man."

"My, that is interesting."

"Is that all you can say?"

"Well, I'm a coward at heart, María. If you told me the details, I'd probably faint."

She raised her wine glass to her lips. "I know you too well, Jack. As a matter of fact, I'd bet that you are the only man I know who could do something like that. You didn't get all those scars on your body from selling arms. You must have used them once in a while."

"María, would you believe me if I told you that just changing razor blades makes my knees shake?"

"Would you believe that I am a virgin?"

We both laughed.

After supper we strolled hand in hand through the narrow streets below the Plaza. In the nineteenth century this area of Madrid was known as The Caves, and it was the haunt of bandits who shot police on sight. Times have changed but The Caves haven't necessarily kept up.

But there are cafés there with the best flamenco singing in Madrid or for that matter Spain, or even the world. Like bullfighting, flamenco is an acquired taste for most Americans. I picked mine up during the heady espionage period of pre-Castro Cuba.

We café-hopped until we found the right place —a bar with a great copper vat of whisky-sodden sangría, a clientele of workmen and a singer with a voice that had the gritty and powerful anguish of a call from hell. Naturally the singer and guitarist were *gitanos*, Spanish Gypsies with faces the color of dark leather and eyes as black as buttons. As they sang, the rest of us beat time on wooden tables with earthenware cups.

"For an American, you have soul," María complimented me.

"That's not all. Come back to my hotel and I'll show you."

The prospect seemed agreeable enough to her, and as I put my arm around her waist, there was nothing further from my mind than the so-called Werewolf. The sangría made us stagger a little, but we staggered together and that's what international friendship is all about. Outside the café we moved along an unlit street and just by chance I saw the flash of two knife blades ahead of us.

From a doorway there stepped two *gitanos*. They wore kerchiefs around their necks, and their hair was wild. Their faces expressed contempt.

Gitanos have quite a reputation for knife work—and a nasty habit of taking a man and breaking his arms, legs, and jaw just for kicks.

"It's very late for you to be out, tourist. You need protection," the nearer one told me as his knife circled the air.

He smiled, displaying a mouthful of gold teeth. His comrade didn't have the same motherlode in his mouth, but a pair of gold earrings in his ears lent him some panache.

I didn't want trouble, and I would have been content to pull my gun and scare them off, but the last thing I needed was curious police on my back.

"Do you want to sell me some protection by any chance?" I asked.

"This neighborhood is very dangerous at this hour," the Gypsy with the earrings told me. "Not even the police feel safe here now, so they leave. I think you should hire us, señor. It will only cost whatever money you and the señora have."

"You don't take traveler's checks?"

They laughed, but they didn't slap their knees. "We will take everything, señor."

They edged us against a wall. No one was coming out of the café, although I did see a Cadillac blocking one end of the street. Whoever was at the wheel wasn't rushing to our aid. One of the Gypsies snatched at María's diamond earrings, and I brushed his hand away.

"No, don't be brave," he reprimanded me and swung the knife under my chin. "Be a quiet little tourist or I'll give you a new mouth across your throat."

"Jack, do as he says. They're killers."

That much I'd gathered. Gypsies in every other part of the world regard the Spanish *gitanos* with fear. These looked as if they would sell their grandmothers, piece by piece.

"Okay, just take my money and get out," I said through my teeth.

That was when the boy with the gold teeth laid his hand over María's breast and squeezed. Enough is enough. The *gitano* with the earrings was guarding me. His hungry eyes were on María's breast. I knocked his knife hand up and slashed the edge of my bare hand across his chest. His sternum cracked like a dry stick, and he rolled into the gutter.

The one with the twenty-four-carat smile was suddenly aware that his friend was whimpering in agony. As fast as a cat, he lunged, his stiletto aimed at my eyes. I ducked under the blade and caught his wrist, using his momentum to swing him off the ground and hurl him headfirst into the stone wall. But he must have had a stone head; he bounced off the wall and tore his arm from my grasp. The blade flashed like quicksilver and sliced through my jacket and into my shoulder holster. If I hadn't been wearing it, I would have joined the first *gitano* in the gutter.

We circled each other warily on the narrow sidewalk. The tip of his knife cut a figure eight in the air as he searched for his opportunity.

53

"Now I will take your money off a dead man, tourist," he hissed. "Your lady will come after."

He would have said more, but my foot shot out and slammed his jaw shut. With both hands I slammed his kidney with the force of a sledgehammer. I backed off before he could straighten up and bring his knife into play.

The *gitano* grinned and spit blood. "*Dios*, you are good, tourist. So now it is no longer a matter of money—it is a matter of honor. For honor alone I have to kill you."

That old Spanish pride. He feinted artfully toward my groin, and as I leaped to the side, the blade followed and stabbed my knee. Another inch to the side and he would have hamstrung me.

"You're not too bad yourself," I admitted.

Six inches of sharp steel cartwheeled through the air as he tossed the knife from hand to hand, pressing me back. It was bait. I was supposed to try to kick it away, and while my leg was up, he would put an end to my love life.

I started to kick but held back. The *gitano* plunged in with his low stab. I twisted to the side and drove my fist down into the side of his face, feeling the cheekbone shatter. He reeled, but he still had his knife, and he was heading for María.

I gathered the back of his collar and his belt in my hands and lifted him high over my head. The blade flailed uselessly as I threw him against the side of the nearest car. As he caromed off, I knicked him back into the air, caught him, and threw with better aim, sending him through the car window. Limp inside the car, his legs sticking up through broken glass, the *gitano* had nothing more to say.

The other Gypsy had picked himself up, out of the gutter and crawled away.

"*Olé*," María whispered in my ear.

Now that the action was over, the Cadillac finally rolled out of the shadows. Very excited, its driver jumped out, full of concern. He was a big, overweight man with pale eyes and a close-cropped red beard. His clothes, snug over a massive belly, were obviously the most expensive a Madrid tailor could produce, and his pudgy fingers flashed with heavy rings of gold and lapis lazuli. His cologne almost made me yearn for Hawk's cigars. I was pretty damned shocked when I discovered that he was one of María's best friends.

"I arrived just in time to see you handle the Gypsy," he swore. "I wish I'd come sooner."

"Me too," I agreed.

The bearded blimp's name was Andrés Barbarossa, and María mentioned that he was a powerful industrialist. He giggled at the introduction.

"And who is this superman?" he asked. "I didn't think anyone could beat a Gypsy with a knife. But you're bleeding, my friend. How stupid of me to ask questions now. Allow me."

As if we were old fraternity brothers, he helped me into the Caddie. Barbarossa obviously knew his way around Madrid. Within a minute we were out of The Caves and he was parking smoothly outside an extra-posh restaurant. One of the delights of Spain is that restaurants stay open almost to dawn. Once inside, Barbarossa led us to his private table and ordered brandy from an obsequious sommelier. María cleaned my small wound with water dipped from a crystal goblet.

"How do you feel now?" the industrialist inquired.

"Napoleon brandy can cure anything but death."

"So true," Barbarossa said and filled the bottom of my snifter again. "Now, reveal your identity, superman."

"Jack is a salesman for a weapons firm," María answered for me.

"Oh," Barbarossa's face lit with interest. "What firm?"

"Swiss Universal. Our headquarters are in Zurich, where a lot of our clients' money is."

"We do buy arms for some of our operations. I don't think I've ever heard of Swiss Universal."

"We're fairly new."

"Small arms?" Barbarossa seemed more than ordinarily intrigued.

"Small arms," I said, "or personnel carriers, field pieces, tanks. Propeller planes or jets. We also hire out advisers on request."

"Fascinating." Then Barbarossa dropped the subject and I didn't pursue it. From this point on, he kept up a polite conversation about my impressions of Madrid. The most I could get out of him was that his business concerns had vaguely to do with "development."

"*La cuenta, por favor,*" he called the waiter and got the check. When I tried to pay, he waved my money off and simply signed the bill.

Barbarossa wanted to drive me to the Palace Hotel but I knew enough about Spanish decorum to put him off and take a cab instead. That way María felt free to accompany me and tuck me into bed.

"I think Andrés is jealous of you," she said as she folded her dress over the back of a chair. "He has a great brain but, unfortunately, not the most attractive physical appearance. He always reminds me of a great, red boar."

"Let's forget about Andrés Barbarossa for a second."

She slipped under the sheets and I ran my hand up her smooth flank, pulled her close so that her breasts spread over my chest. We kissed, our tongues entwining.

"God, Jack."

I rose inside her. The *Naked Maja* flashed through my mind. This was what her smile was all about.

María's legs embraced me, pulling me in. Her hands cupped my face, holding it still and kissing it as our bodies rocked together.

I wanted to forget about Barbarossa, but I couldn't completely put him out of my mind because when he signed the check, the double "ss" was written with the Teutonic runes of the SS.

That's the trouble with mixing business and pleasure.

CHAPTER SIX

I was having a late breakfast in the Palace dining room when the telephone was brought to my table. Just as I hadn't been able to forget about Barbarossa, he apparently hadn't been able to forget about me.

"How are you feeling this morning?" his voice asked, full of solicitude.

"Just a bad cramp in the leg, thanks."

"Very good. You know, I was very impressed with the way in which you protected our friend María. It also happens that I am in the market for some small arms. Do you think you're up to a plane trip?"

"Where to?"

"Just a hop to Morocco. It would take a few days, no more. If you care to make a sale. . . ."

My cover as an arms salesman would look pretty

damn strange if I didn't. I calculated that Franco's schedule wouldn't take him out of El Pardo for another week. He would be safe for the time being. As for concluding a real arms sale to Barbarossa, I had no worries about that. There really was a Swiss Universal firm in Zurich, as I was sure my telephone caller knew by now. AXE doesn't leave loose ends.

"No trouble," I said. "What kind of goods are you interested in? I'll bring some samples."

"Automatic rifles. I'll have my car pick you up at three this afternoon. It will drive you to the airport, and we can go together in my plane."

"Perfect. I'll be looking forward to it."

When you've been an agent for as long as I have, you may not grow any special antennae, but you do develop sensitive skin. Mine told me I was being watched. Barbarossa wanted to see me contact someone and if it wasn't Swiss Universal, then the fat industrialist would know I was more than a salesman.

My problem was to figure out whether Barbarossa was just a nasty rival for María's interest or a real lead to the Werewolf. True, he'd sat by and let the Gypsies get off their best shots at me, but I can name about seven million people in New York City who would have steered clear, too. And true, he'd signed his name with the telltale SS but that might be pure coincidence. In which case, I'd look pretty damn silly leaving the country.

I called Zurich. The AXE agent who answered

the phone carried on as if he were nothing more than a clerk in an office and I was a salesman. I hung up and finished my breakfast coffee with my first cigarette of the day.

It was bright and sunny as I left the hotel. A bellboy, a pair of priests, and a flock of businessmen followed me out of the lobby. On my right was a broad avenue. I took a small street to my left and lost the priests. All along the street were small perfume shops and art galleries, catering to tourists. The bellboy stopped off in one of them, apparently running an errand for one of the hotel guests.

I skipped across the street, weaving my way through the traffic of Vespa scooters and small Seats, Spanish-made Fiats. When I was a block closer to the Plaza del Sol, I noticed that one of the businessmen crossed the street after me.

At the next corner I turned in a rush and then stopped short as if I had a great interest in a window full of lingerie. My shadow whipped around the corner and almost bumped into me.

"Excuse me," I said in an amiable fashion.

"Excuse me," he answered in kind.

I strolled down the street while he took his turn examining the lingerie. When he looked up, I had disappeared.

From the doorway I'd slipped into, I heard his footsteps hurrying closer. I caught him in midstep and yanked him into the doorway.

"Excuse me again," I apologized as I pressed the tip of my stiletto into his spine.

"What are you doing?" he blustered. "There must be some mistake."

I found his belt holster and liberated his gun.

"Nope, no mistake. Who sent you?"

I had him pressed into the letter boxes. He twisted his head around and began to sweat a little for me.

"Who? I don't know what you're talking about."

"I'm not going to kill you, you know. I'm not that kind. So I'll just lean on this knife until it separates your spine and you're paralyzed for the rest of your life."

"Wait!"

That meant he wanted time to think up a good enough lie.

"I'm from the *policía*."

"Not good enough."

I leaned on the knife tip.

"Wait, I'll tell you the truth."

But he didn't. He turned and elbowed the knife up. It would have been a fine move if I'd only had one hand. I countered with a left cross. His head snapped back into the mailboxes, and he crumpled to the marble floor.

When I knelt down over him, he'd already stopped breathing. I pulled his jaw open and the odor of almonds escaped from his mouth. Cyanide, not nuts. He'd been carrying the pellet in his mouth all the time, and my punch did the rest.

That's one reason I hate fanatics, it's so tough to get an answer from them!

I put some distance between myself and the

doorway. I knew I hadn't taken care of the Were-wolf, but at least I was free to pick up my sample.

Pawnshops everywhere in the world have signs with three gold balls. The one I went to off the Plaza de San Martín even had the usual international display of watch fobs, guitars, and clarinets.

"I lost my ticket," I told the clerk, "but I remember what it was I left."

The clerk was completely bald and made up for it with a grandiose mustache that was waxed to daggers.

"I don't remember you leaving anything," he lisped in a Castilian accent.

"An ax with the number three burned into the handle."

"Oh, that ax." He stroked his mustache. "I think I have it right here."

As usual, the AXE network had been thorough. As soon as the man at Swiss Universal hung up on my call, he'd contacted our "safe house" in Madrid and told them what I needed. While I was dispatching my shadow, the package was being delivered to the hock shop drop point. If you're wondering how you can get such good telephone service in Spain—you can't. AXE's illegal tie-lines bypass all of Europe's incompetent telephone systems.

"Everything is satisfactory, I assume."

I opened the case he pushed over the counter. It was no ax, but it was satisfactory.

"There's another package I'd like to pick up in

a few days," I said. "A rundown on Andrés Barbarossa."

"If you don't pick it up?" he asked.

"Then I want that man killed."

CHAPTER SEVEN

"Curious thing happened to me today," I remarked as Barbarossa's Lear jet hurtled across
the Mediterranean and he and I sipped whiskey
by the plane window. "A man followed me from
the hotel. I can't understand why."

He smiled and his red beard bristled.

"I always heard that selling arms was a cut-
throat business."

"Oh, no," I assured him. "It's just like selling
insurance."

His belly jiggled as he laughed.

"I'm sure you underrate yourself, Mister Finley.
María told me about your fighting the bulls. You
see, I have met many soldiers of fortune. That's
what you are."

"Not since I got an expense account."

"Delicious, delicious," he wagged his head. "I

don't know when I ever met anyone with such a sense of humor. We'll do a lot of business together, I'm sure."

The jet passed over the African coast without losing altitude.

"You see, I run a mineral consortium in the Spanish Sahara, Mister Finley. Mostly wolfram and potash. You understand their uses, naturally."

"Tungsten from the wolfram and potassium from the potash. Lamps, drills, ammunition, paints, and potassium cyanide. Just to mention a few."

"You're well informed. In any case, valuable commodities. As some other African nations are somewhat envious of our control, we must constantly be on guard against so-called guerrilla saboteurs. I have a sizable guard handling the problem, and to cover our investment, I must have the guard well equipped. Especially since we began expanding our operations."

"Expanding?"

"Yes. You'll remember I said we were going to Morocco. We are exploring for potash there, and since it will take time for the mining operations to start, I am using our holding as a camp for our guard."

"A camp? That must be a pretty big guard."

We had passed Tangier, and ahead lay the Atlas Mountains.

"There's one American saying I have always liked," Barbarossa said as if he were confiding a secret. 'Think big.' You like that saying, don't you?"

"Sure. It just means a bigger sale for me."

Potash, hell. They weren't going to find any potash near the airstrip we landed at. The field was carved into the mountains sixty miles from the Atlantic coast and midway in a wilderness between the Moroccan cities of Rabat and Fez. I may not have been close to the Werewolf, but I was sure onto something. As we approached for the landing, I saw a military camp big enough to train ten thousand men.

The Lear touched down in a perfect landing. Plumes of smoke trailed after the jeep that drove out to meet us. I could have sworn the captain at the wheel was going to salute Barbarossa until he saw me.

"Mister Finley is here on a business mission. But that can wait until tomorrow."

And it did. We were driven to a guesthouse on a side of the mountain facing away from the camp. At supper I was the guest of honor as women in veils brought out great silver plates of cous cous, partridge in plums, and lamb baked in cinnamon. The other guests were the higher officers of Barbarossa's private army.

"Does it surprise you that we live in the Arab style here?" he asked me. He had changed after the flight into the gownlike djellaba of a Berber.

"It may surprise me, but I like it," I said as I rolled a tasty ball of cous cous between my fingers.

"Always keep in mind that it is said Africa ends at the Pyrenees," Barbarossa orated. It was clearly a thought close to his heart, and I let him ramble.

"For seven hundred years Spain was ruled by Arabs. Every city in Spain has a castle, but what is it called? The *alcázar*, an Arab word. Where did the Generalísimo make his reputation? In the Sahara, with the Spanish Foreign Legion. What turned the tide of the Spanish Civil War? Franco's arrival with his Moors. Spain and North Africa are indivisible."

His officer corps reflected that. There were some Nazis and French, to be sure, but most of the officers were Spanish and Arab, and it was in these two groups I saw the fire of fanaticism.

One of the latter, an Arab with a hatchet face, chimed in enthusiastically, "Can you imagine the power if Spain and North Africa joined again? It would mean control of all Europe and Africa."

"A tempting thought," Barbarossa jumped in, "but most improbable. Besides, our guest is not interested in politics."

The tables were cleared and water pipes were brought out. The sweet smell of the smoke told me hash was mixed with the tobacco, not an unusual habit among expatriate officers.

The serving girls were replaced by dancing girls who had none of that bare-midriff routine handed out in the nightclubs of Casablanca. These girls were fully clothed in silk gowns, gowns that nearly burned right off them as they went through the most explicit contortions of lovemaking. It was all strictly look-don't-touch, but enough to give one dreams of more than sugar plums.

Reveille was at seven. Bugles and stamping feet. One of the dancing girls came into my room and threw open the doors to the veranda. There, where the bougainvillea tumbled in scarlet clumps down the wall, I had chilled juice and poached eggs. My guess was that the soldiers were messing on hash and biscuits. I was willing to trade.

Barbarossa joined me before I'd finished. "Forgive me for not eating with you," he apologized, "but I make it a habit to eat with my officers. To build the esprit, you know."

The industrialist really took to being a make-believe general. Instead of business suit or djellaba, this morning's masquerade consisted of khakis and combat boots. I tried not to seem too interested in the uniform's shoulder emblem—gold braid coiled around the twin lightning bolts of the SS.

He took me on a personal tour of the mining site. There was excavation work going on, and an unusually large number of heavy crates were lined up outside the mine entrance.

"Drills and boring equipment," Barbarossa explained.

I had the honor of eating with him and his officers at lunch. We were seated in an immense prefabricated mess hall, where I had my first real look at Barbarossa's soldiers.

When he'd said he knew soldiers of fortune, he meant it. Every veteran from the Bay of Pigs,

Algeria, Katanga, Malaysia, and Yemen seemed to be present. It was a convention of killers for hire. None in the Werewolf class but good enough to skin anyone trespassing on the Barbarossa empire.

"What campaigns did you say you took part in?" a German major asked me as he passed the carafe of wine.

"I didn't say."

"Come, come, Jack. You must recognize somebody here," Barbarossa prodded. "Perhaps an old friend."

I understood his tactic: verify my status as nothing more than a traveling salesman or catch me in a lie. If I were a salesman for weapons of death, it would follow that I'd used them from time to time. The table's attention was turned to me. The wine didn't spill as I poured it out.

"Not unless you have some of New York's finest here," I drawled. "I was a cop, not a soldier."

The major guffawed. He had a squat pig nose and tiny, blue eyes. The tattoos rippled as he slapped his muscular arms on the table.

"A cop! A common cop is going to sell us rifles? I never knew a cop who wasn't made of rabbit drops."

If any hospitality was being injured, Barbarossa didn't acknowledge it. He urged the major on.

"So you don't think much of the salesman, Erich?"

"I like a man who knows what he's talking

about. All a cop knows is slapping whores and swinging a club. What does he know about rifles?"

The whole mess hall was riveted to the officers' table by now.

"Well, Jack?" Barbarossa asked me, "Major Gruen has a very low opinion of you. Aren't you insulted?"

I shrugged. "The customer is always right."

But Barbarossa wasn't so easily put off. "Jack, this involves more than your honor. He says you can't know anything about rifles. Now if I am going to buy rifles from you, I'd like to think that you did know what you were selling."

"A demonstration," Gruen bellowed. "Let him give a demonstration on the parade ground."

The entire mess hall emptied as the men picked up on the major's suggestion. Barbarossa's scenario had been well prepared. My case was waiting for me on a table, erected in the middle of the dusty field. Gruen watched me open the case, a sneer covering his ugly face. The regiments of soldiers sat down in a great circle as if they'd come for a prizefight.

I lifted the automatic rifle high for all to see. "This is our standard recoil-operated weapon. A G-3. It fires the NATO standard 7.62 mm calibre cartridge—there is never any problem in procuring ammunition."

The G-3 is a good enough weapon, too. It's heavier than the American M-16 but less apt to jam. No doubt most of the men listening had used it in action.

"How does it operate?" Barbarossa asked, like a good student.

"When the trigger is pulled, the hammer fires the bullet. The explosion not only fires the bullet, the gases produced propel the cartridge case and breach block blackward, forcing the sealing rollers against the sloped shoulders of the bolt until the bolt is disengaged. As it moves, the breech block extracts the cartridge and cocks the hammer. A spring moves the block back forward and strips a new cartridge from the magazine, ready to fire. The G-3 can be adjusted to fire automatically or in single shots."

"Very good, very good. You memorized that well," the German applauded. "Now show us." He grabbed a handful of cartridges from the ammo box and stuffed them into the magazine. Then he shoved the G-3 back into my hands and pointed to one end of the parade ground where dummies, used for bayonet practice, hung from a rack.

"There are three dummies. I'll give you four shots to put them on the ground. Otherwise, you are a liar and not fit to lick scum."

"And if I do ground them, what are you, *mein Herr?*"

The blood rushed to Major Gruen's face. He rubbed his hand over the hip holster of his Luger "Grosser." The Grosser is one of the largest handguns ever built; most men can only fire it as they would a rifle, using a wire shoulder stock.

"This gets more amusing all the time," Barbarossa smirked.

"Fire," Gruen ordered.

The soldiers standing between me and the dummies moved out of the line of fire, so that an avenue of spectators almost spanned the hundred yards to the rack.

I fondled the G-3, getting accustomed to its weight. No one made a sound. I got the stock comfortable on my shoulder and then lined up the rifle sights on the right of the three cloth dummies.

My first shot cracked the silence. The dummy swayed slowly.

"Nowhere near the rope," Gruen laughed. "He never used a rifle before."

"Odd, he usually knows what he's doing." Barbarossa seemed disappointed I'd missed so badly.

I hadn't, though. I'd aimed at the dead center of a dummy's belly. The hole I'd put through it was an inch to three o'clock. It's good to know that sort of thing before you get serious.

The soldiers were clapping in derision. Barbarossa relaxed and lit a Cuban cigar. Gruen slapped me on the back and roared.

"Shoot away, salesman. If you drop the dummies, I will be the first to say what a fool I am."

"Is that a promise?"

"A promise, salesman."

I snatched the rifle back to my shoulder. Between two of Gruen's breaths, I squeezed off three shots. Two dummies lay on the ground. Then the third rope snapped in half and all the dummies were stretched out in the dust.

I ignored the German and placed the rifle in Barbarossa's hands.

"How many did you want?"

The Spaniard gazed steadily at his major.

"A promise is a promise, Major Gruen. The salesman has made a fool of you. We're waiting for you to say it."

"Dummies don't fire back!" Gruen sputtered in protest. "So he can fire a rifle. Any coward can shoot dummies." All the German's instincts rebelled against this humiliation. Not only his employer but all his subordinates were waiting for him to admit he'd made an ass of himself. Better death than dishonor. "Leave him to me, and in two seconds I'll have him crying for his mother. If he has one."

Unfortunately, some of my instincts were being aroused at this point. I'd had enough of Major Gruen.

"All right, you unreconstructed Nazi swine. You'll get what you want. Clear the field, señor Barbarossa. I'll give you a real demonstration, since that's what the major wants."

I outlined the terms of the demonstration. Both Gruen and I would disassemble our weapons—he the Grosser and I the G-3—and the first one capable of firing would do so. And kill the other.

"But yours is a much more complicated weapon," Barbarossa pointed out. "It's unfair."

"Leave that to me, señor."

Gruen grinned at my confidence. We paced off a distance of thirty yards while some of the officers took our weapons apart. A near-holiday air pervaded the parade ground. This was more amusement than the soldiers expected and exactly the kind of entertainment they could appreciate.

The major squatted, his great hands ready to put together the ten simple pieces of his Luger. Next to me was a pile of springs, the stock, breech block, magazine, hand guard, flame arrester, barrel, trigger mechanism, grip, sights, firing pin, hammer, and the thirty-odd screws that hold a G-3 together.

Along the sidelines the soldiers made bets. The odds were ten-to-one against me, which meant one in eleven soldiers was pretty smart.

"Ready?" Barbarossa asked.

Gruen nodded eagerly. Then I nodded, too.

"Go!" Barbarossa called.

Skillfully Gruen began putting the Luger together. The magazine into the handle. Trigger, trigger level, roller, and catch into the breech block. Hammer snapped in from the top. He stood and aimed.

The G-3's heavy bullet tore out the center of his chest. He landed ten feet back of where he had stood and lay there with his knees up and spread, like a woman awaiting her lover. But Gruen wasn't waiting for anyone anymore.

I held the bare tube of the barrel, breech block, and the loose spring I'd used to pull the hammer back. The rest of the rifle was still lying on the ground. Since the automatic action had slipped a cartridge into the breech after firing at the dummies, I hadn't even had to use the magazine.

"When I said it was unfair, I was obviously thinking of the wrong man," Barbarossa observed. "Too bad, he was a good officer."

"Dumb. He was dumb."

"No, he underestimated you, Mister Finley. That's something I won't do again."

The episode cut short our stay. Barbarossa thought some of Gruen's friends might try to take revenge, and he said he didn't need any more dead officers.

I was eager to go, too. I'd overheard two of the soldiers discussing the news that Franco had suddenly decided to make one of his rare tours of Spain, probably to quiet rumors of his assassination.

If the Werewolf had anything to say about it, Franco would end up proving the rumors.

Barbarossa and I took off in his jet before supper. He was deep in thought, but then abruptly he clasped my hand.

"How much do you make as a salesman? I'll double it if you'll take Gruen's place. I need a man of your talents."

"No, thanks. Playing soldier in the middle of nowhere isn't my idea of fun."

"Trust me, Jack. It won't be that way for long. You'll see lots of action, and the rewards are greater than you'd ever imagine."

"I'm flattered but you'll have to be more specific. I never was one of those who joined the Navy because someone said I'd see the world."

"See the world? Shake the world, Jack. We are poised on the point of action right now. I can't tell you more than that."

We left the sky over the mountains and coasted toward the Mediterranean, a lone spot in the air for camelherders to gawk at.

"I'll think about it, then."

Thinking about it put it mildly. As soon as he said his operation was poised to move, I realized why he had his base in the middle of the mountains. Only ten miles from the phony potash mine was the secret American communications center at Sidi Yahya. His men could take it over in one rush and cut off Washington's communications with the Sixth Fleet, which was patrolling the Mediterranean.

He wasn't just aiming at Spain but at Morocco and control of the Mediterranean. Werewolf was just the primer to an explosion that would make Barbarossa a new world power or escalate into a world war that neither America nor Russia wanted.

CHAPTER EIGHT

Franco's first stop was Seville. Seville's *feria*—spring fair—is the first big event on the Spanish calendar, and every hotel room in town is reserved months in advance.

During the day Arab horses pull carriages with señoritas dressed in traditional costumes. Crowds flock into pavilions to watch flamenco dancing and no one goes without a glassful of sangría or sherry.

"Not even the Generalísimo can stay away," María boasted. Ronda is not far from Seville, and she had fierce local pride in the *feria*.

"I can't stay away from you. That's why I came. You're much more attractive than your friend Barbarossa."

"Oh."

We were in a pavilion that sheltered us from

the fierce Andalusian sunshine. She swept two glasses of sherry from a waiter's tray and handed one to me. Over on the dancing platform high-heeled flamenco shoes were beating on the floor.

"What did you think of Andrés?" she asked.

"It's hard to know what to think. He offered me a job, but he wasn't very specific about it. Besides, I like being my own man. You don't have any idea of what he has in mind, do you?"

"Me?" Her fingers touched that irresistible cleavage between her breasts. "All I know is brave bulls and brave men. I have no idea what Andrés is up to."

I was happy about that. Before coming to Seville from Madrid, I had made my return call to the hockshop, where I'd picked up the report on señor Barbarossa. Until the age of thirty he had been nothing but the younger son of an aristocratic but poverty-stricken family. That was when he got his first lucky break—heading up a South African mining corporation in the Congo while Tshombe was riding high. When Tshombe collapsed, Barbarossa got out with company stock certificates, worthless pieces of paper that he was able to parlay into millions in cash through a shady mutual fund in Switzerland. From there he spread out into real estate and politics—and then took possession of Spanish mining interests in the Spanish Sahara after having the previous owner blackmailed until he committed suicide. By the time I met him he was one of the most powerful men in

Spain, and tomorrow . . . ? Well, Andrés Barba-rossa was clearly thinking hard about that.

María cocked her head.

"Are you sure you're back on vacation, Jack? You're always thinking about something else. Concentrate on me. You know, a countess can have any man she wants."

"Consider me your slave."

"That will be the day."

When dark fell, the main event of Seville's *feria* began—a procession of thousands of religious clubs throughout the city. The members dressed in capes and high, conical masks like the ones the Ku Klux Klan wear. Holding their candles, they turned the city into an eerie fairyland.

Those not holding candles bore gigantic floats carrying religious statues, figures of Christ, the Virgin Mary and the saints. Franco himself was to review the floats from the steps of the Cathedral of Seville. To those of us watching, the procession seemed a river of candles carrying these fantastic idols out to sea. With the final touch of fireworks bursting in the sky, this is probably the most inspiring and unnerving spectacle in the world.

Especially for me. The Werewolf could be any one of the thousands of men in capes and masks parading before me. I could just see the General-ísimo, a feeble figure at the top of the cathedral stairs raising his hand weakly to the cheers of the crowd.

"Have you ever seen anything like this?" María asked as the crowd jostled us back and forth.

"Never."

Fireworks exploded over the church, casting a green light. Then red and yellow ones followed. At any second I expected a different sort of bomb to erupt on the steps.

Nervously I opened my cigarette case and spilled the contents on the ground. "Damn. I'm going to have to get some others."

"Not now, Jack. The good floats are just coming."

"I'll be right back."

She protested, but I had to get away on any pretext. I forced my way through the crowd, searching for a better vantage point.

A float with a black madonna stopped in front of the cathedral steps. A man in the crowd began singing to it, an emotional, wailing serenade that drew shouts of approval from the listeners. Even Franco applauded.

I strained my eyes for a sign of the Werewolf. There were dozens of floats, and there was no possible way I could check them all.

"I wonder what church that float is from," the woman next to me whispered to a friend.

"It's new to me," the friend answered.

The approaching float didn't seem new, just larger than most, with a mammoth figure of Saint Christopher bearing the Christ child over a river. A human machine of men in red capes carried it closer to the church.

"Aren't all these floats supposed to be traditional?" I asked the woman.

"Yes." She hoisted her camera. "I can't wait to get a picture of it."

But I had the picture. I made my way through the crowd to the rear of the Saint Christopher float. The serenade to its predecessor was ending and the "new" float would be reviewed next by Franco.

The serenade ended, and the red robes started forward. I slipped under the rear end of the float and crawled toward the front.

The red capes shuffled toward the Generalísimo on each side of me. Peering out, I could see the churning legs of the police and the crowd. There was no one under the float but me. I crawled faster than the legs walked until I was directly beneath the statue.

The statue was hollow and there, perched inside of it, was the Werewolf. He held a submachinegun tight against his chest, his eyes pressed to a slit in the chest of Saint Christopher. At the right moment I knew that the statue's chest would fall open and the Sevillanos would see fireworks they'd never forget.

Already the feet of the crowd were distant, and I realized that we were in the square right in front of the cathedral. The Werewolf's hands twisted tensely around the submachinegun. From somewhere in the crowd a serenade for Saint Christopher began, and María looked around for her missing salesman.

I pushed myself up into the statue and grabbed the Werewolf's legs. He was younger than I'd expected. I took him by surprise, and he tried to kick me away, but I only pulled at him all the harder.

The statue wobbled as we struggled. The Werewolf twisted on his perch and swung the submachinegun barrel down to fire. Before he could, I forced my way into the statue's cavity and trapped the rifle, nose down, between us.

"Bastard," he grunted. "Who are you?"

"Give up."

It was like fighting in a coffin. We could barely move, but he managed to get his hands around my neck. I discouraged him with a straight-fingered stab in the kidney. Suddenly the hollow statue was stinking with the sour perspiration of fear.

His thumbs jabbed at my eyes. I twisted my head back and forth, but his fingers pushed their way into my sockets. I couldn't get enough arm room to shake my knife from its holster or to reach my gun. What I did do was ram my head forward in a butt that knocked the wind out of the Werewolf.

While I was trying to focus my eyes, he found a straight razor somewhere. I saw the flash of the blade and ducked within the confines of the statue. He missed me, and a chuck of wood flew up from where the blade landed.

I couldn't get my arms up to protect myself. The razor slashed again and again at my throat, each time missing by a smaller margin. Finally, he held my neck steady as he stabbed. As the razor struck at my jugular, I let go and dropped from the statue onto the street, flat on my back. The Werewolf had won.

The submachinegun barrel protruded from the statue, aimed at my face. I kicked it up desperately. The Werewolf's finger was already pressing on the trigger as the barrel swung back up at him. Obviously, it was on automatic fire.

I rolled to the side as a shower of blood and wood poured down from the hollow statue. An arm and a leg hung down limply. The submachinegun was wedged between the dead would-be assassin and the statue, propping up the lifeless body. There was little left of the killer's chest, and his head was no longer human.

I waited for the rush of police, half expecting a blast of gunfire that would finish me. Nothing happened. Only then was I aware of the cannonade of fireworks exploding overhead, which had completely muffled the deadly fire of the rifle.

"Move on," a parade marshal shouted as the fireworks ebbed.

In some confusion the red capes resumed their movement. Once the float was back on a crowded street, I slipped out. I knew that one of the red capes would crawl down under to see why the assassin had lost his nerve. They'd find he'd lost a lot more than that.

CHAPTER NINE

Most Americans think of sherry as something you put in lentil soup or that awful stuff you refuse to drink when you visit grandma. It's true there is a sweet, tepid kind that fits that bill, but in Spain stevedores will fight over an insult to their *manzanilla*, a dry, nutty sherry that's served from the cask in neighborhood bars. There are bars in the rougher sections of Spanish towns that serve nothing but sherry and a licorice-flavored brew of firewater called anise, and together the sherry and the anise make a boilermaker with megaton power.

I was learning these facts with Colonel De Lorca, head of Spanish Intelligence. It was just an hour after the Werewolf's death, and the *feria* was still going on. De Lorca was a slim, dark man about my age, with an aquiline nose offset by an almost-comical Fu Manchu mustache. He was dressed casually in civvies.

"They ran from the float as if it had a bomb in it—most disrespectful." He bit into a salty olive. "At any rate, we rounded them up and found the assassin. Frankly, I was rather surprised."

"Why?"

"Oh, I'd expected something different. Just a bunch of run-of-the-mill radicals. But a good enough scheme—I give them credit for that. Without you, it might have succeeded."

"Might have? What would have stopped it?"

"Me." De Lorca seemed surprised he had to explain. "If you ever get to read the official report, you will find that while you were of some aid in detecting the assassin's strategy, it was I, Colonel De Lorca, who assumed the physical dangers. Don't look so irritated. Hawk will get something nearer the truth. It's not so much that I want to steal your glory but that I want to save my neck. If the Werewolf had as much as missed the *Caudillo* by a mile, the next day would have seen a new hole in my family cemetery plot. It's a fact of life."

A fact that might have explained his cynicism and why he was tossing down the Spanish boiler-makers.

"You're supposed to be pretty good, De Lorca. They wouldn't kill you just because an assassin got too close."

"After that stunt you pulled at the Royal Palace? For two generations Spanish society has been built on one foundation—Generalísimo Franco. He falls, everything falls. Señor, he sneezes and the state trembles. I said, '. . . if you ever get to read the official report . . .' because the report will be secret. No one will ever know. We, the professional officers, will carry on to the end like priests of a dying god because we know that our world ends with him. Well—Killmaster versus the Werewolf! It must have been a good fight. *Salud*."

We raised our glasses and drank. De Lorca sighed and stood up.

"I have some reports to fill out. You don't have to come along; you've done your job."

Back on vacation, I found María at Seville's most exclusive nightclub.

"Where have you been?" she pouted. "What mysterious errand did you go off on this time?"

"I thought I saw an old friend. I was wrong."

"You missed Andrés. He was asking for you."

"In that case, let's get out of here."

María's idea of hiding out was to accept an invitation to one of the *feria* parties being thrown by Seville's oldest families. With a small crowd of Italian princes and Rumanian duchesses we piled into a Rolls and drove off into the dark. The Rumanian duchess on my lap reminded me of an overblown Zsa Zsa Gabor. With every bounce of the road her bosom enveloped my face.

"Where the hell are we going?" I shouted to the front seat where María rode.

"To Jerez."

Jerez? Jerez was hours from Seville. I couldn't

believe I was going to be in the perfumed embrace of the duchess that long. Wrong again. By the time I rolled out of the Rolls, I was willing to trade the Rumanian powder puff for a return bout with the Werewolf.

"Look, María, I was thinking of something more private than this."

"Come on, Jack. You'll never see another place like this."

Perhaps she was right. The villa was actually a sprawling estate, a Gothic mansion in the middle of thousands of acres of vineyards. The driveway was jammed with raucous petty nobility from every country in Europe. It must have been a bit like this in Russia right before the revolution, I thought sourly.

Despite the late hour, the lords and ladies were determined to make a party. Underneath mammoth portraits of fierce-looking conquistadors and scowling admirals, a mass orgy was getting into swing.

"I'd always heard that European nobility was incestuous. I didn't know this was what they meant."

"Don't be a prude, Jack."

"Oh, I have the same inclinations. It's just that I have a stronger sense of privacy."

Our host appeared. He was a white-bearded marquis of something-or-other in a velvet jacket.

"Jack is bored," María said. "Why don't you show him the wine cellar?"

I thought she was kidding, but the marquis reacted with tremendous excitement.

"A great pleasure. It's so rare that I have a guest who can keep his clothes on." He glanced with a jaundiced eye at the rest of the party.

"Why do you have them, then?"

"See that great ass dancing on the table? That's my son."

We went through a series of dining rooms until the three of us reached an immense wooden door, built into a wall that was decorated with men in armor. The marquis took out an ancient iron key.

"There is another entrance from the vineyard, but I always use this one. Since sherry built this house, it only seems right."

He led the way down a narrow stairway. When we reached a stone floor, he turned the lights on.

Wine cellar was hardly the description for what lay under the house. Row after row of enormous wooden casks filled a cave. "Sherry" is the poor English translation of *jerez*, the wine of the city of Jerez, and the marquis was one of the great sherry-growers in Spain.

"How much wine do you have down here?"

"Each cask holds fifty barrels. In all, I believe we have a hundred thousand barrels or so. Half is for export, and most of that is *oloroso*, very sweet, and what in England and America they call cream, also sweet. The rest is *fino*, fine sherry, either *amontillado* or *manzanilla*. Here."

We stopped beside a cask the size of a small

elephant. The marquis held a cup under the tap and loosed a stream of amber liquid.

"The fortune of a sherry house depends on one great year. From then on we blend every other crop with it. How do you like it?"

I sipped. The wine was powerful and musky. "Damn good."

"It should be. My family pressed that over a hundred years ago."

We did a lot more tasting. It was an alcoholic's vision of heaven. Casks were everywhere—the wood branded with the wine's type and age. Whiskey is a distillery product of alcohol, charcoal, and caramel coloring. Sherry produces itself by aging for at least seven years in the special wood of the casks.

Just then a servant came down from the house to tell the marquis that his son wanted to talk to him.

"Please remain if you like," the marquis told us. "There is no reason you should suffer what I have to."

María and I still had some cups left untasted, and we sat down to do the honors on a ramp that led to the vineyard.

"Now aren't you glad we came?"

"It's very educational," I agreed.

Suddenly I heard the door to the house close. I expected the marquis to reappear but it definitely wasn't the old man.

Two musclebound, unfriendly types came down

the stairs. In their hands were broadswords taken from the marquis' collection of armored men.

"María, did I say something to insult your friends?"

"No, Jack. I can't imagine what these men want."

I recognized them now as two of the chauffeurs who had driven the cars from Seville. They seemed to recognize me, too, because they began running toward us as soon as they spotted us.

"Hold it!" I yelled and reached for my Luger. It wasn't there. The duchess. During all that bumping and squeezing, she had stolen it. Obviously the drivers knew I didn't have it because they kept running, their five-foot-long broadswords held over their heads.

"María, the old man said there was another door out of here. Make a run for it."

"What about you?"

"I better slow them down as best I can."

While María ran up the ramp, I prepared to meet the party's most unwelcome guests. I still had my stiletto, and I shook it out of my cuff to match their steel. The trouble was, of course, that there was no way I could get inside the range of their swords and use the dagger.

When the closest one was ten feet away, I snapped my hand and the knife flew in a line right at his heart. It bounced instead of sticking. Armored vests—they'd taken all the precautions. Rather than waste time thinking about the situation and chance having my head cut off, I dove between two casks and crawled to the next aisle.

"Shut the vineyard door, Carlos," one of them whispered. "Then we'll flush out the American at our leisure."

I pulled my sock down and unstrapped the gas bomb taped to my ankle. Somehow I knew that no one was going to leave the orgy upstairs to come to my aid.

"Here he is."

A broadsword sliced down at my shoulder. I threw myself at its side but the flat part of the sword still grazed my arm. It hung limp and numb. The gas bomb rattled over the floor out of reach.

The sword came sideways at my waist as if to cut me in two. I ducked and a gusher of sherry poured out of a cask onto the floor. The killer swung at my fet, and I jumped up on the damaged cask. Just as the tip of the broadsword jabbed up, I jumped over to the top of the next cask.

"He's a ballerina, not a killer," the chauffeur laughed.

I thought I was on vacation. What the hell were these two men trying to kill me for?

There was one on each side of the cask now. Their swords clanged together as they tried to pick me off. I jumped across to another cask.

"You can't dance forever, ballerina. You may as well come on down."

The broadsword is a primitive instrument but it's effective. In the hands of a strong man it has the cutting power of a mechanical scythe. Richard the Lionhearted once stood off an Arab army by cutting in half every champion the infidels could send up.

The men rocked the cask and I slipped between it and the cask next to it. I was pinned there, hanging like a bayonet dummy. My feet dangled uselessly as half a ton of pressure crushed my chest.

"Got him!"

I pulled my hand back. The sword sliced into wood where my wrist had been. From the other side another sword hacked close to my thigh. It's one thing to be shot down in a fight—it's another to be picked to death while you're being crushed like a stupid turtle under a steamroller. And not even know why. . . .

Somehow I drew my legs up and pushed. Every muscle in my legs and arms strained as I heaved the mammoth casks aside. The one at my back budged grudgingly. It wasn't full; I could hear the wine slopping around in it. Encouraged, I sucked in oxygen, shouted the muscle-liberating karate "Ha!" and forced the casks apart. I scrambled back on top before my audience could believe their eyes or hack off one of my legs.

"I thought only the Werewolf could do something like that," one of them said.

I jumped over his head and into the aisle. The sword arced after me, too late. I found my knife and ran.

"Force him toward the vineyard door," I heard one of my pursuers shout.

My legs were wobbling after the strain of pushing the casks apart. Instinctively I ducked and felt the air whisper as a broadsword bashed into the cask I was passing. The miss gave me a lead of a few more feet. The strain of swinging the heavy swords was telling on the men too. They were slowing down.

I half-ran, half-crawled, up the ramp to the vineyard door, right to where they intended to trap me. I went around the cask at the top of the ramp and jammed my knife into the lock. It didn't give.

"Will you come down here, or do we have to come up there after you?" one thug shouted from the bottom of the ramp.

"Come on up," I gasped, figuring that way I might be able to face them one at a time.

"It doesn't matter."

Single file, they started up the ramp. I turned and slashed the rope by my side.

They stopped, thinking I must be going mad with fright. Then they saw the rope traveled over a pulley and around the cask. Their eyes grew as the rope parted and the cask lurched off its blocks.

"No!"

They tried to run back down the ramp, carrying their heavy swords. If they had dropped the unwieldy weapons, they might have had a chance but a thousand-pound cask of wine gathers speed awfully fast. The whole basement shook with the force of the rolling cask. The thugs disappeared underneath it, the swords flying out like toothpicks. Their screams were muffled by the rumble of the cask. Like a steamroller, it flattened the killers and continued on into the first row of casks.

A flood of sherry spilled out over the stones as the rolling cask split open. The wine washed over the two inert bodies. They were both dead, their bones crushed.

If they hadn't been afraid of making noise, they would have used guns and I would be dead. If they hadn't been afraid of bashing in too many casks with their swords, they wouldn't have chased me to the vineyard door and I would be dead. Two mistakes too many.

I dipped my finger into the sherry that was running over the floor and tasted it.

Amontillado. Vintage 1968. A good year.

CHAPTER TEN

"But why would they want to kill you?" María asked.

"A damn good question."

We had returned to the safety of our hotel room in Seville. And I had switched from sherry to scotch.

"A rival in the arms business?"

"No. Mistaken identity, maybe."

"Who would they mistake you for, Jack?"

"You're full of good questions."

I wished she had more answers. Such as why nobody would come to help when she told them there were two killers in the basement. I know I'm a commoner and all that, but I'd think a murder would take the edge off any orgy.

"France is really going to be succeeded by a monarchy made up of those clowns?" I wondered aloud. "It seems to me that any strong man with nerve could brush them aside with a handkerchief."

"Perhaps that's why they play so much—they know they have so little time left. Maybe that's why I play with you—I know we have so little time too."

I pulled down the zipper of her dress. Her black hair fell to her waist. I pushed it aside and kissed the nape of her neck. As I slid my hands around her breasts, I felt their tips growing hard and sensitive. She leaned back into me and took a deep breath of pleasure.

"Your vacation has to end sometime. Then I'll go back to the ranch or Madrid and in a couple of years I'll be married to some idiot of a lord. Or a man of money."

"Like Barbarossa?"

"He's asked."

"And that's not what you want?"

She turned to face me, her lips parted.

"You know what I want."

I eased her onto the bed. While I pulled her dress off, she unbuckled my belt.

We'd made love before but never with the intensity of that night. Her lithe body became a machine of unending pleasure, her desires as urgent as a countess in heat. Again and again I drove deep into her as her back arched to receive me. The bed rocked with our love. When I was milked dry, she used her fingers and lips to revive me, and when it was finally over, we fell asleep in each other's arms.

The next morning I contacted Colonel De Lorca and we met on the banks of the Guadalquivir in the middle of Seville. At one time the river held the Spanish Armada, but now it's almost a dry bed, like modern Spain.

"Where does Franco go from here?" I asked.

"We drive to the Mancha so he can do some pheasant hunting. He's an avid hunter. Why do you ask?"

"Two men tried to kill me last night."

"They failed, apparently."

"Thanks. Unfortunately, they're dead, so I can't ask them what it was all about."

"I will investigate it."

Sea gulls flew up and down the river, scavenging like rats with wings. They didn't find much.

"That's not what concerns me, Colonel. I think the Werewolf is still alive."

De Lorca shook his head. "He's dead, Killmaster. Dead ten times over."

"The man in the float is dead, you mean. How much chance of escaping would you have given him after he killed Franco?"

"No chance, of course. It was a suicide mission."

"Right. Now how many cool professionals plan suicide missions? None. There aren't many ways you can spend your payoff in the grave."

"You have a point. Do you have any other reasons for believing the Werewolf is still alive?"

I flexed my stiff legs. "During the fight last

night, I happened to get stuck between two casks of wine."

"Embarrassing."

"And also very uncomfortable, with two men trying to stick swords in you. The point is that when I got free, one of the thugs said he thought only the Werewolf could do anything like that. I doubt very much that they could have given us a lead on the Werewolf's identity, but I do think they must have seen the Werewolf at one time, and he must have given them an impression of great physical strength. The man in the float— how big would you say he was?"

"Five-nine, five-ten. Wiry."

"But no Hercules."

De Lorca thought about it and nodded. "Agreed. So you have two implications that you killed a spare assassin and that the main danger still exists. Let me put your mind at rest. I have not been as idle as you think."

"You went to this party last night with the contesa María de Ronda, did you not? You are, shall we say, intimate with her. Your rival, don Barbarossa, is a very jealous man. He is also very wealthy and powerful and he owns the company of chauffeurs the killers worked for. I can tell you all this out of general information. Now use your common sense. What better reason can there be for killing you than to remove you from María de Ronda's affections? These things are not uncommon here. America is a more cold-blooded country.

"As for the Werewolf. Could he have escaped from the casks of wine? Perhaps not the way you did—through strength—but why not through agility? You yourself found him a formidable opponent within the confines of the statue.

"Could he have escaped after assassinating Franco? I say he could not because I would have been sure to kill him. Sad to say, however, I cannot answer for the loyalty of everyone in the Generalísimo's entourage. Possibly, even the police on hand would have protected the assassin instead of killing him. That's why I used such secrecy in asking for AXE's assistance. No, you've done your job. Now you should relax and enjoy yourself and keep out of Barbarossa's way."

Barbarossa. If De Lorca thought my ideas about the Werewolf were off base, what would he think of my suspicions concerning the industrialist's private army?

"Tell me, colonel, is there any truth to the idea that Spain and North Africa have more in common than Spain and Europe—that Spain and North Africa have some sort of special ties?"

The Fu Manchu mustaches lifted with amusement. "Don't you know what the name of this river was originally, Killmaster? It was Wadi el Kibir. We just changed it to Guadalquivir. Our churches are remodeled mosques, that's all. You don't have to scratch Spain very deep to find Africa."

A sea gull found something on the opposite bank. At once other gulls were on top of him, trying to tear the food out of his beak. Isn't this what would happen to Spain when the old dictator dies?

"Franco was never aware of the attempt?"

"Never. He's a little hard of hearing, anyway, and what with the fireworks . . . he heard nothing. You did it perfectly." He looked at his watch. "Which reminds me, our cars are leaving soon, and I must be with them. I will have someone look into the chauffeurs' attempt when we get back to Madrid. Good luck."

There was nothing I could say that would stop him. His arguments that the Werewolf was dead were convincing enough. And I had only a half-formed theory about the plans of Andrés Barbarossa.

A figure waved to me as I climbed up the steps from the river bank. It was María.

"Who was that I saw you talking to? Another salesman?" she inquired as we met.

"Yes." I lied with a straight face. "He's in lingerie. Selling it, I mean. I wanted to get something nice for you."

"Hmmm. That sounds as if you're going on one of your little trips that you never tell me about. Just when the bullfighting season is really getting started and we see the best fights of all in Madrid. Tell me you'll come. You can't just drop me and pick me up every two seconds."

"I wish I could."

She glared at me. Hell hath no fury like a woman scorned, and María was an aristocrat.

"If you run off this time, don't bother coming back."

"I'll meet you in Madrid."

She stamped her foot in fury. "And you won't even tell me where you're going?" she pouted.

"Bird-watching. Now what could be safer than that?"

CHAPTER ELEVEN

I ate a cold omelet, and peasant bread, washed the food down with wine, and watched the clouds roll by. A brisk wind traveled over the flat plain of La Mancha. From time to time I rolled over on my stomach and trained binoculars on the road.

After an hour the helicopters came. They passed, a mile overhead, crisscrossing as they searched for intruders. I pulled some brush over me and waited until the copters passed. As they went on, I watched them with field glasses. Huey Cobras, part of Franco's protection.

I heard the sound of tires. On the road three landrovers appeared and behind them came a truck full of peasants. The convoy came to a stop not far from me. While the men from the landrovers gathered around a tureen of coffee, the peasants spread out over the plain. In a traplike formation they set off on both sides of the plain, beating the brush with poles in order to drive birds and rabbits to the center. It was in the center that Generalísimo Franco would wait for his prey to show.

Submachinegun-toting Guardia Civil followed the peasants, alert for any strangers the Cobras might have missed. Franco and company sat on hunting sticks, patiently sipping their coffee. If the Werewolf was still alive, I saw no sign of him.

I felt not so much that I was protecting a modern dictator as that I was trespassing on a nineteenth century painting of a hunting party. Peasants with beating sticks, the Guardia Civil in their tri-corner hats, Franco in English hunting tweeds. It was all out of a time machine.

The boom of a rifle broke the rural silence. One of the hunters had taken the first shot, apparently at nothing. Beside Franco stood an adjutant with a selection of small-calibre rifles and shotguns.

A rabbit bounded past me, and behind him I heard the sound of a beating stick. I dug myself deeper into the underbrush. Luckily, the peasant's attention was fixed on the rabbit as he passed me only three feet away. I relaxed and studied the hunting party again with my glasses.

The Werewolf was running out of opportunities. He would have to strike soon. As Hawk had advised, I'd been putting myself in the assassin's shoes. An analysis of Franco's recent tours of Spain showed that he always started out with a grandiose itinerary through the nation's cities and then cut off the tour at midpoint. The fact was that Franco was not welcome in Barcelona, Bilbao, Santander, and other major cities because of festering ethnic complaints in these towns. The Catalans of Barcelona were denied use of their own dialect, and there was a small guerrilla war heating up among the Basques of Bilbao. Another reason for Franco's shortened trips was that he simply ran out of energy. Each time he cut off a trip it was right after a hunting trip—if the Werewolf didn't strike today, he might not get another chance.

On the other hand, what better time to strike than during a hunting party? One extra crack of a rifle wouldn't be noticed until the dictator fell to the ground.

The ring of beaters was closing in. Most of the hunters were standing and firing. A slaughter of pheasants and small game was taking place close by the landrovers. Franco remained seated, apparently bored. When the fusillade was over, the peasants strung up the bleeding game by the feet, and the day's entertainment was over.

Hunters and beaters piled back into their landrovers and truck, and drove off. I remained there, lying on my face in the middle of nowhere.

After they were out of sight, I got to my feet and strolled over to the road. The small village where Franco's party was staying was at least ten miles away. I trudged toward the town, feeling like a complete fool.

An old peasant rode ahead of me on his burro. He was in the patched shirt, corduroy trousers, boots, and black hat that all the farmers in La Mancha seem to wear. When he turned at the sound of my footsteps, I saw his face was tanned and leathery, with a white bristle from not having shaved for days. His gray eyes were speculative and intelligent. He stopped and waited for me to catch up. Finding conversation in La Mancha is not easy.

"*Hola!* Where are you bound?" he asked in the coarse dialect of the region.

Dressed in deliberately shoddy city clothes, with a bandanna tied around my neck, I answered in the dialect of Seville. "To San Victoria. Am I on the right road?"

"You're a sevillano. No wonder you're lost. Come with me. My burro and I are headed there."

We walked together in silence for a while until his curiosity got the better of him.

"Do you know what distinguished visitor we had here today? Did you see nothing unusual?"

"A helicopter. I've seen helicopters before in the city."

"So what did you do when you saw this one?"
"I hid."

The old man laughed and slapped his leg.

"A sevillano who tells the truth. This is an unusual day. Well, brother, you were wise to hide. Those were helicopters of *El Caudillo*. He was here today shooting."

"No!"

"I'm not a liar by trade. My brother was beating the bushes for him—my cousin, too. A great

106

honor but of course it ruins the hunting for the rest of us who need food to eat. You understand, this is not a criticism of the Generalísimo. I have never criticized him."

"Not much," I thought. To add to his lack of credibility there was a fat pheasant hanging from his burro.

"You don't seem to be doing too bad."

"Oh, that. I caught that in my snares. I wonder if any of the generals shot one as fine. Perhaps when we get to San Victoria, I will make a present of it to our leader."

I wouldn't want to take odds on it. The old man was like peasants the world over, more cunning than a Wall Street broker.

Talking brought thirst. We stopped and shared squirts from his goatskin wine sack. I angled my squirt neatly down my dry throat.

"Have you ever seen a tourist trying to drink from one of these?" he chuckled. "First in his eyes and then down his shirt. I always make it a point to offer wine to tourists. For a hundred pesetas I will even pose."

Finally we reached San Victoria. The old man saluted me with his cap.

"I leave you here but with some advice, friend. The town is lousy with *policía*. You know the Guardia Civil—shoot first and ask questions later. The farther you put yourself from the Generalísimo, the safer you are. Maybe his helicopter didn't see you the first time, but it will the second."

"I understand. Thank you."

He wiped the sweat off his face with his sleeve. "Incidentally, what are you doing out here in La Mancha?" he asked.

"Looking for work."

He lifted his eyebrows and tapped his head, signifying that I must be crazy. "God go with you, friend. You need all the help you can get."

The old man was right. You couldn't take a step in San Victoria without landing on the boot of a Guardia Civil. A dozen pairs of eyes followed me down the main street. The church was the biggest building in the village, and soldiers lined its roof.

I turned off the main street and found a small café. It was doing a lively business, serving lunch to many of the men who had been beating the bush for Franco. For the equivalent of ten cents I got a bottle of harsh red wine and a plate of stew.

By eavesdropping, I learned that the Generalísimo had had a stomachache during the morning and that was the reason he hadn't shot. But he was feeling better now, and an afternoon party was being arranged. Many of the peasants were disgruntled by the news.

"I have to go back to the farm."

"So do I. This afternoon it is my turn for the irrigation water. You know what will happen if I don't get any water."

"This is an honor," a fat man wearing a better quality flannel shirt than the others said. "You can't leave now."

"My family should starve for the honor?"

"The honor of the village."

"Your honor. You're the mayor," one of the farmers told the fat man. "That's fine for you. What about the rest of us? You can always get some boys to beat the bush."

No matter how much the mayor blustered, half of the farmers refused to go out for the afternoon's shoot.

"Well, I'll remember this," he threatened them. "You."

I looked around for the man he was talking to.

"You there. The stranger."

"Me?" I pointed to myself.

"Yes, you, stupid. You can beat the bush, can't you?"

"I suppose so."

"A sevillano," he sneered. "You also expect to be paid?"

It would have been too abnormal not to. "A little something," I suggested meekly.

"Fifty pesetas and the meal for free."

I glanced at the farmers. One of them made a raising motion with his hand.

"I don't know."

"All right. Eighty pesetas. That's all, or I'll have the Guardia arrest you as a bum."

So much for Spanish unions. The mayor rounded up some of San Victoria's boys, and after the generals had had their siesta, we climbed into the truck for the afternoon's hunt.

The landrovers led us to a different part of the plain, one strewn with boulders and snakes. Of course, the shooting party wouldn't have to worry about that since they would be sitting in the clearing the whole time. Franco's helicopters zoomed about like giant flies buzzing in the hot sun.

The line of beaters I was in fanned out to the left. Every ten feet a rabbit or a pheasant would spring from the brush and run pellmell to its doom. After fifty yards of traversing the rubble, I stopped and knelt down.

"Go on, I'll catch up," I told the boys nearest me. "I have some rocks in my shoes."

"City shoes," they pointed out. "You should have boots out here."

The line moved ahead while I emptied my shoes. In a couple of minutes it was out of sight.

"What's the matter?" a vaguely familiar voice demanded.

"Rocks in my shoes."

"Stand up when you talk to me."

I stood. A Spanish foreign legionnaire poked my chin up.

It was Scarface, the bodyguard I'd already met twice at the Royal Palace. Once I was in the Special Effects disguise, though, and the second time was during our fight at night in the ballroom. I counted on that.

"You're beating the brush for the Generalísimo?" he asked skeptically.

"Yes, sir."

He was in khaki desert gear. As he walked around me, he slapped his leg with his rifle.

"Haven't we met before? Have you ever been in the Legion?"

"No, sir."

"You're big enough. You don't look the sort to me who goes beating the bush with farmers. I never forget a face—you're sure we've never met?"

"Maybe in Seville. I'm from Seville. You might have seen me there."

He rubbed his scar. "No. Somewhere else. Well, at any rate, you've fallen far behind. Catch up with the rest if you know what's good for you."

"I will, sir."

The burly legionnaire's face froze. Confusion gave way to nasty certainty. I looked down at the ground. I'd turned as I'd spoken my last words to him, and seeing my face in shadow, he recognized the face he had seen in the ballroom.

He had no doubts now. "I remember you, señor. Yes, I've been looking for you. I owe you something from that night at El Pardo. And when I'm through I'll do what we in the Legion always do to traitors—bring in your head and stick it on a pole."

"I don't know what you're talking about, señor."

As soon as he started to answer, I kicked the rifle out of his hands but his hands weren't empty for more than a second. Scarface slashed at my neck with a knife. I caught his arm, locked it at the elbow, and threw him over my shoulder. He bounced back to his feet, still holding the knife.

"Ah, you do know what I'm talking about, as-

111

sassin, don't you? All the better when I cut your heart out."

He swung, and I caught his arm again. But this time he shifted his weight and threw me fifteen feet over the ground.

"I killed my first man when I was fourteen," he boasted. "I was the strongest man in the Legion when I was seventeen. You don't have any pianos to hide behind this time, so you have no chance."

"Don't forget, I was hell in the Boy Scouts."

While confusion clouded his face, I jumped and gave him both heels in the forehead. The kick should have staggered a horse, but the veteran legionnaire tackled me around the waist and slammed me down on the ground. With both hands he forced the edge of the blade to my throat.

"Stop gulping and you won't feel a thing, boy," he whispered.

The muscles of his shoulders bunched as he forced my arms down. The blade was already moving in a sawing motion. At that point I held his wrists still. At first he couldn't believe his wrists were locked, that his arms were overpowered by mine.

"You are no farmer," he gasped.

His scar turned white, and blue veins stood out along his neck but he couldn't break the stalemate. I twisted his hands to the side and the knife plunged into the ground. As he fell forward with his momentum, I rolled him over on his back. Now I was on top and the knife was in my hands.

As slowly but as inevitably as a watch's second hand approaching the numeral six, I brought the knife down to the legionnaire's neck. I sank my weight into it, bulling his hands down. The knife tip touched the hollow at the bottom of his neck.

A spray of dust filled my eyes. Overpowered and admitting it, Scarface had thrown a handful of dirt in my face. I coughed blindly. The knife struck the ground futilely. I felt the legionnaire rise from the ground and step around me.

A second later a cord wrapped around my neck and snapped taut, choking me. No air got through and I began to gag on my tongue.

It was a garrote, the favorite Spanish execution. In jails they do it with a wooden collar and screws. In the Legion they do it the old way with a cord. Very effective. My heart raced for the oxygen it wasn't getting. Already the lack of it had my brain ready to go comatose. I made sick, retching noises as he jerked the cord tighter.

Then I held onto the cord with both hands and pitched forward. Scarface flew over my head and onto the ground. Still choking, I heard him scramble to his feet. Blindly I kicked with all my might where I judged his most vulnerable spot would be.

The blur that was Scarface wavered. Inarticulate noises of agony came from his gaping mouth. Clutching his scrotum, he collapsed to his knees. I unwrapped the garrote from my neck, exposing a raw red ring of flesh. I resisted the temptation to wrap the cord around Scarface's neck.

"Think of it this way," I told him, "you won't have to eat saltpeter for months."

His moans were growing louder. I picked up the rifle and swung it like a four iron under the base of his skull. Scarface stretched out on the ground, unconscious.

I let tears wash the dirt out of my eyes and then I exchanged clothes with the legionnaire. I knew I couldn't find a better disguise for moving freely around the periphery of the hunt. And the hunt was in full progress. The beaters were closing the ring on the panicked animals. The boom of guns came at shorter intervals.

I found a boulder and climbed it for a vantage point. Through the glasses I saw Franco being helped from his seat and being given a gun. I knew that I could be seen from the landrovers, but in the Legion uniform and flat kepi, no one would notice me.

A rabbit dashed across the shooting ground. Franco selected a light-gauge shotgun as deliberately as a new tie and fired. The rabbit somersaulted, landing on its back, dead.

Not bad for a man in his eighties.

The other shooters applauded. Franco waved them to silence and selected more shells from his shooting case. He was well known as a hunter, and I guessed that he was choosing shells that had a tighter pattern of shot. I could easily imagine his staff loading his rifles with wide-pattern shot just to make his hunting easier, if a bit on the cheap side. The same way Eisenhower's secret-service men would regularly kick his golfballs out of the rough and onto the green. It used to drive Ike crazy, but they wouldn't stop.

The hunting party seemed to be headed for as drowsy an afternoon as the morning was. A pheasant exploded from the bush. Feebly Franco led it with the sights of his rifle. He fired, and the bird dropped. More applause.

Most of the beaters were sitting and watching by now, their work done. An occasional dispirited *"olé!"* rose from them while the Generalísimo shot.

I scanned the horizon. Nothing but boulders and underbrush. In the far distance a windmill. Then, as I was about to drop the glasses, a flicker of movement where there should have been none.

Almost directly across from me, on the other side of the shooting party, was a line of boulders. One of them wasn't right. It had a burro's ears, ears that twitched with each report of Franco's gun.

I squinted through the underbrush around the boulders until I made out the hunched figure of a man. It was the old peasant I'd traveled with to San Victoria. The adrenalin stopped pumping. Obviously, curiosity about the Generalísimo had overcome him—and he probably wanted to see his brother, too.

A pheasant exploded from the brush where he crouched and took to the air. The bird gained altitude and flew toward the shooting party. Perhaps the old man was making a present to the *Caudillo*, after all.

One of Franco's adjutants pointed the bird out. Franco took a freshly loaded shotgun and aimed. The pheasant flew straight toward him, passing no more than fifteen feet over his head. One barrel fired and then the other. Untouched, the bird went by and turned in a circle, wheeling around over my head.

Incredibly it turned back toward the shooting party. Cries of excitement came from the hunters as they spotted its return. Franco grasped a new gun.

The pheasant flew stiffly, unnaturally. As it neared the Generalísimo, I studied the bird through the glasses. The head was rigid, the eyes unseeing. It was no more alive than a stuffed dodo.

I whipped the glasses back to the old peasant. Anxious about the pheasant, he'd dropped all pretense. He half-stood, his fingers turning the dials of a radio transmitter. He was the Werewolf. I'd spent the morning with him and this afternoon I would witness his assassination of Franco.

The fragile dictator led the bird with his sights. It flew directly at him, an impossible-to-miss target with wide-pattern shot but not so easy with a tight-pattern shot, because heading directly at you presents a smaller silhouette.

Franco fired. The bird seemed to hop in the air but it was due to the air turbulence around the shot. The second barrel fired. Unbelievably the fake bird flew right on through.

Angrily Franco snatched another rifle. It had to be wide-pattern shot this time. The hunters called encouragement as the bird began to turn again.

Hunter's luck, they must have thought.

I swung back to the Werewolf. Unflustered, he was directing the pheasant back on a third pass. The artificial bird was radio-controlled but the bomb wasn't. I calculated what kind it would be— a pound of gelatine in a gunpowder sack planted in the mechanical bird's chest. One pellet would set it off and they'd be lucky to find Franco's shoes.

The flying bomb wheeled for its last approach. It would flutter just slightly over my head. I aimed the legionnaire's rifle at the hinge of the bird's right wing.

The Werewolf must have spotted me. The pheasant suddenly dipped and my shot went high. I ejected the cartridge, fired again and missed. The bird danced right over my head and soared down toward the hunting party. If I shot and missed again, my bullet would continue down among the hunters.

I aimed at the fat chest of the bird and squeezed the trigger.

A light as bright as the sun exploded on the plain. The rifle flew from my hand with the force of the blast. I felt myself tumbling through the air in a dreamy, slow-motion dive, but when my shoulder and head hit the ground, the impact was plenty fast and hard. I skidded on my face and hands for about fifty feet, the thorny under-brush clutching at my skin. I tried to keep count of my arms and legs as I rolled.

I hit the boulder like an egg hits the floor.

CHAPTER TWELVE

A dream. A weary, narrow face at the foot of a bed. A colorless mustache, liver spots. Respectful conversation. Myself silent. Finally, the visit over, putting on a hat with a bill oozing gold trim.

Then doctors. Bandages. By the bed, bottles with tubes. Tubes in my arm. Sheets rustling like the feathers of a mechanical bird.

Awake. I sat up in bed. In the dressing-table mirror I saw the reflection of a big, dark-haired man in a hospital gown—Nick Carter—and not looking too chipper. De Lorca was there.

"Welcome back," he said from a chair beside the bed.

"From where?"

"From wherever you've been."

"How long?"

"Comatose for the last three days. Don't bother. You have all your toes and fingers. It was the concussion. Nothing permanent except a jellied brain and some first-degree burns, although we thought you might have a detached retina or two. Quite a sight when we picked you up, though."

He rose from the chair and pulled back the window drapes. Outside I could see the traffic jam of the Puerta del Sol. We were in Madrid. De Lorca smiled his Fu Manchu smile.

"You had blood coming from your eyes, ears and mouth. Definitely not a dish to set before a king."

"Thanks for the compliments, but I've got work to do."

He pushed me back down on the bed. "You've got some resting to do. The doctors still can't figure out how you survived."

"Spanish doctors?"

"As a matter of fact, Spanish Air Force doctors. Most people would have been torn apart by the gravity strains you went through. They say you're a beautiful specimen."

"Of the living or dead?"

"In between. But I'm serious when I say you have to rest." He picked up the chart at the end of the bed. "Fever, abnormal blood pressure, possible blood clot, one lung almost collapsed, hemorrhage of small blood vessels."

"In other words, nothing I couldn't expect from

standing under a bomb. Nothing at all. I think I'd rather be an out-patient."

"Please," his hands were on my chest again. "Hawk will send a bomb if I let you go out the day you leave your coma. Besides, you have some explanations to give me."

I told De Lorca about the Werewolf and his trained bird. I was glad to see that the colonel was the sort of intelligence officer who was capable of receiving information without writing it down.

"He's good, this Werewolf," I said in conclusion. "I swallowed his disguise hook, line, and sinker. He'll be back, too. You should have seen him with that transmitter. A cooler assassin I've never seen. He's just been delayed, not stopped."

"Did he get a good look at you?"

"I'm afraid so. My cover is blown as far as he's concerned. Speaking of being blown, how is that legionnaire?"

"The one you almost emasculated?" De Lorca smiled. "He's in the next room. I think it's just as well we don't tell him where you are." He tugged on a mustache. "You know, nobody ever beat him hand-to-hand before. Maybe the Werewolf is good, but you live up to your reputation, too."

My eyelids kept sliding down, and a torpor spread through my body. "I see you put a sedative in the glucose."

De Lorca came in and out of focus. "The more you rest, the less chance of shock. Don't worry, the Generalísimo will be at his palace tonight.

We'll go out there together tomorrow. He still wants to talk to you."

"Was . . . was he . . . . ?"

"That's right. Franco was here while you were comatose."

De Lorca said more, complimentary, no doubt, but I faded from consciousness. My head sank back into the pillow, and I was asleep.

It was night when I opened my eyes again. I looked at the dressing-table clock. 10 P.M. My stomach growled with hunger, a sure sign of recovery. I found a button hanging by my bed.

A doctor answered the call.

"No nurses?" I asked.

"This is a very restricted ward." He read my chart and slipped a thermometer in my mouth.

I took the thermometer out.

"Why the face mask? Am I contagious?"

"Please put the thermometer back," he groaned. "You may not be contagious, but I have a cold."

He checked the bottle of glucose hanging over the bed. It was empty. He put a full bottle in its place. I took the thermometer out again.

"The reason I called was because I'm hungry. You know, food that isn't intravenous. Something for my mouth to work on."

He shoved the thermometer back in.

"Antishock procedure means no solid foods. Apparently you don't even comprehend that you shouldn't be alive after what you went through."

He opened the tap of the new bottle. A clear stream of liquid ran down the tube into my arm.

The doctor's accent was Madrilenian, but it seemed somehow recognizable.

"What does the official report say happened?"

"Seems you interfered."

That made me sit up.

"Interfered? What the hell do you mean by that?"

The doctor looked straight at me for the first time. He had gray, intelligent eyes. The same eyes as the old peasant in La Mancha.

"You. The Werewolf."

"And you, Mr. Carter. I knew they would send the best after me. I thought it might be you, although I wasn't sure of it until tonight. Let me congratulate you on your performance with the pheasant. I'd congratulate you on your luck also, but I'm afraid that's run out."

"My luck? You're the one who's trapped in this hospital. You. . . ."

My tongue felt thick. I blinked my eyes hard to concentrate. "You're the one who's. . . ."

I couldn't make my lips coordinate. My fuzzy gaze swept up to the bottle dripping into my arm. "Sodium . . . pen. . . ."

"Sodium pentothal. Exactly," the Werewolf nodded. "A sloppy truth serum but a very effective general anesthetic. I knew they would have some on hand."

I tried to pull my arm free of the tube, but somewhere between my brain and my arm the order got lost.

The Werewolf pulled down his mask. The old

man's grizzle was gone. The face was younger, leaner. "When the Spanish lost the courier in the plane crash, I knew someone had to show up. I figured it would be an English agent or one from the CIA. Then when the dead man was found in the float, I said to myself, 'Nick Carter.' I knew it was your kind of handiwork, no one else's."

He pressed the button three short times. "You fooled me back in La Mancha. You do dialects as well as I do. You simply have to be taken out of the way. If the Russians put as high a price on your head as they say they do, you'll be a nice bonus."

"A nice bonus," I heard and the rest of his words were lost in a buzz that ran through my brain. I was vaguely aware of a sheet being placed over my face. Of another man entering the hospital room. Of being placed on a mobile table and being rolled out.

I had stopped the Werewolf from assassinating Franco, but I couldn't do a thing about his killing me.

CHAPTER THIRTEEN

The first hint I had of being alive was the smell of animals. It wasn't just the odor of dogs but the strong, pungent smell of beasts. I couldn't see anything because a canvas sheet lay over me, but the buzz was gone from my brain, and I could move my fingers freely. I was dressed in a shift and pants.

It didn't make sense; I should have been six feet under by this time. Either the Werewolf had changed his mind or he had been forced to dump me alive. The only thing bothering me was the powerful animal stench.

I raised the canvas. The Werewolf hadn't made any mistakes.

I was in a bullring corral with six fighting bulls. These weren't calves like the one I'd fought on María's ranch but true, full-grown killers, monsters twice the size of calves, with horns more than three feet across. The nearest one was almost stepping on me.

Very slowly I turned my head and looked for the gate. It was on the other side of the corral, on the other side of six huge bulls. Without doubt it was locked from the outside. I wasn't going to get out that way.

The corral walls were whitewashed adobe, fifteen feet high, with no purchases for a hand or foot. There were no exits. The Werewolf's trap was perfect.

The bulls grazed on a thin scattering of fodder. Like fighters, they would go into the ring hungry. They seemed peaceable enough, an effect of being together in a herd. Shortly before the day's fight they would be separated and put into individual pens. The trick was to stay still until the corral keepers came to do their work. Only the trick was an impossibility. Bulls don't have the best of eyes, but they do have very good noses.

A roan monster pushed fodder with his muzzle. A black bull spread his legs and released a stream of urine. Another sharpened his horns on the corral walls. By the end of the day each of these incredible killing machines would be dead, but now they were kings.

One stepped over the canvas and scratched his muscular hump on the wall. The roan bull chewed, his long tongue licking his pink muzzle. Another bull walked in front of him and stopped.

I had to restrain myself from swearing. On the

flank of the nearest bull I saw the brand—a jagged SS. The Werewolf had an unpleasant sense of humor.

That wasn't my worry, though. The roan bull came closer, like a vacuum cleaner mindlessly cleaning up loose pieces of hay. Through a slit between the canvas and the ground I saw his large eyes roaming over the sheet.

What would the corral keeper think when he arrived and found my body? Not much. It wasn't unusual for aspiring amateur bullfighters to invade bullring corrals and try out their skills on the waiting beasts. The mortality rate of these stunts was a hundred percent. I would be just one more dead fool.

The red bull almost had his nose under the canvas by this time. His tongue slid over the ground; then it touched my hand.

He snorted and stepped back. The other bulls whipped their heads around and stared at the canvas, their ears erect. The one or two that were lying down got to their feet.

The roan returned to the canvas and dug his horn under it, tentatively jabbing my ribs. The tip of the horn was as sharp as a stiletto. Then the monster bellowed and tore the canvas cover off of me.

The effect on the other bulls was electric. This was what they had been brought to the bullring for—to kill a man. If they were merely murder weapons, it made no difference to them.

I pulled my shirt off to use as a cape. I knew

how ridiculous my chances were, but a dirty white shirt was all I had to use. There was still some sodium pentothal in my system, but the racing adrenalin quickly overcame it.

The red bull, all half a ton of him, charged. I waved my shirt at his eyes and drew him to the side. His shoulder hit me and drove me into the wall.

As I bounced off, the second bull, a black one with a crooked horn, was already charging. The straight horn swung at my head. I ducked and staggered to the center of the corral.

The third bull charged from the rear. I twisted out of his path and fell to my knees. A fourth monster charged down on me. He followed the shirt. His rear hoof kicked me in the stomach and knocked my breath out.

None of them bellowed or pawed the ground; there were no signs here of a coward. These were the best. I forced myself to my feet and passed the fifth bull. He thundered by and drove his horns deep into another bull. The order of the herd had been broken.

The bull with the horns in his chest fell and screamed. He twisted his head back and forth, but death was fast clouding his eyes. Blood spurted onto the ground, making it slippery and warm.

The roan ran over me and dragged me against the corral wall. I held onto his head as his horns stabbed for a clear shot. When he backed off for a better charge, I rolled over the ground.

The stench of blood filled the corral and inflamed the bulls. They were a chaotically charging mass, trying to kill each other as well as me. Another bull was down, gored. He heaved himself up and swung his horns, willing to fight until he was dead. The havoc was only a momentary reprieve. Being penned in a corral with five crazed bulls was no lease on life.

A horn struck my head from behind and pitched me onto the ground. Horns sliced open the hard earth around me. I turned on my back to look up at a pink snout, red-tinged eyes and twin bayonets of horn. A hoof pinned me where I lay.

Suddenly, the roan was screaming and rolling on the ground. A black bull stood over him, digging out his intestines. The corral grew warmer, more fetid. When the black bull was finished with the roan, he turned to me.

As María had said, a thousand years of careful breeding had made them the mad killers they were. I remembered those words and what she said about the fighting bulls' origin in Crete. The Cretans hadn't been bullfighters, though—they'd been bull leapers.

The black bull charged, his head down. I threw the shirt at his eyes and jumped. It may not have been in the classic Greek manner, but I landed with one foot between the bull's horns. I pushed off its round shoulder hump with my other foot and leaped for the wall.

The bull was nearly six feet tall at his shoulders. There were nine feet between me and the top of the wall. I stretched and grabbed the rim with my hands. As I heaved myself up, the black bull tossed the shirt out of his eyes and charged at my dangling legs. Hunks of adobe shot off the wall.

He was too late. I pulled myself up and hung onto the top of the wall. The bull turned and faced the others. Only two were left alive. One was bleeding from the mouth. The other two charged him, driving him into the wall. His horns swung around desperately, catching the black bull by the neck. They tore at him and battered him into the wall. The three bulls were locked together. They stumbled into the wall below me, shaking it with their strength. As the black one dropped, one of the other two flew over him flush into the wall. I slipped off, met a reaching horn, and swung back up.

Only two were left now. They squared off in the center of the corral, their tongues hanging with fatigue. At some invisible signal they charged each other. The collision of their heads was like the report of an artillery gun.

They backed off and charged again and again. Dizzy, their muzzles bleeding, gore matting their hides, they locked their horns and twisted. Finally one was giving way. It fell to one knee and then the other. The victor sank his horns into the downed bull's soft underbelly, ripping at it until his horns threw tissuelike, damp, dripping confetti around the corral walls.

Then he sauntered to the middle of the corral

—triumphant, ruler of all he surveyed: five dead bulls and four close walls.

I dragged myself along the top of the wall, moving away from the corral. As far as I was concerned, he could have it.

CHAPTER FOURTEEN

A double scotch and a lobster sautéed in sherry made me feel human again. I waited until evening to pay my last respects at the Madrid villa of Andrés Barbarossa.

It could be a trap every bit as deadly as the bull corral, but I had a couple of reasons to think I had some chance of survival. The Werewolf in all his boasting had not once mentioned my cover as Jack Finley, arms salesman. This fact didn't necessarily mean that Barbarossa had no suspicions—it could simply be a result of the loose contact between the assassin and his employer—but I had to find out. Most important, I still didn't know for sure whether Barbarossa was the man behind the plot.

His villa was a mark of his rise in the world. It was a marble Renaissance mansion, set in a private park off the Avenida Generalísimo. Personal guards loitered around the garden, and the driveway was cluttered with limousines. Barbarossa was giving a party.

The butler gave me some grief when he couldn't find my name on the guest list, but Barbarossa himself appeared and ushered me in. He was full of himself, strutting like an overweight rooster. In a ballroom I saw several industrial magnates and their wives with diamond tiaras, plus a heady sprinkling of military men.

"How very lucky that you came by tonight," Barbarossa confided. "The situation is coming to a boil. You have decided to join us?"

"I still haven't made up my mind."

"Perhaps I can convince you."

He led me into the ballroom. A violin quartet provided live Muzak. Magnums of champagne sat in buckets of ice.

"This is the cream of Madrid society," the industrialist murmured proudly. A chubby, cheerful-looking man in a tuxedo adorned with medals rose to greet us.

"Señor Rojas, this is a new convert. The one I spoke about when I told you of Gruen."

"So pleased to meet you," Rojas cooed in Spanish about as native as apple strudel. He was either ex-Wehrmacht or South African. More than one Nazi had seen the end coming before Hitler and had moved their savings to Switzerland and their addresses to Spain. "You will take Gruen's place?"

"He is twice the man Gruen was," Barbarossa

promoted me like a theatrical agent. "No offense, I know the major was your aide during the war."

"Old wars are gone," Herr Rojas said. "We look to the future."

Barbarossa and I glided to another settee, where a Spanish general in dark glasses shook our hands.

"Andrés talks of you a great deal," General Vásquez remarked. "I wonder sometimes how much he tells you."

"Very little."

"Good. I believe discretion is not his strongest point."

I understood the general's pique. Because of María, Barbarossa said more than he should when he was around me. He had to impress me, to show himself the better man, and if possible, seduce me into the position of taking orders from him. Emotion was interfering with his judgment.

Vásquez I remembered as one of the original Falangists, a Fascist from the start and a member of Franco's cabinet. He could lend respectability to any coup. Conversely, he had the most to lose if a coup failed and he was implicated.

The general removed his glasses, the better to stare at me. "A real estate transaction of this size is not a subject to be bandied about with anyone we happen to meet. We are not the only promoters interested in Morocco. Silence will lead to success."

"Exactly," Barbarossa concurred.

"I will socialize now," Vásquez said. He made it sound as if he were about to walk on water.

I met some other officers, various industrialists of a dozen nationalities, wives, mistresses, and royalty. The royalty could talk only for a moment before rushing back to the free buffet. It didn't matter. I was in a daze.

Real estate developments? If Vásquez wasn't being coy, I was on the wild-goose chase of all time. And either the general's reprimand had hit home or real estate was the name of their game because Barbarossa was suddenly full of facts and figures about the growth potential of the North African tourist market.

Certainly not all the guests at his bash could be conspirators in an assassination plot. Most were the usual slackjawed upper crust you find in any capital city. Exquisitely dressed, beautifully mannered, and absolutely brainless. The main topic of conversation was the mysterious death of the six bulls that had been scheduled to fight in the Plaza de Toros.

"Bored?"

It was María, arm in arm with the most unintelligent-looking nobleman in the lot.

"It wouldn't be very polite for me to say so."

"Juan, will you get me a glass of champagne?"

Her escort bounded off like a trained dog.

"You are bored, Jack. If you'd remembered to call me, you wouldn't be."

I offered her a cigarette. While it lit it, her dark eyes penetrated the flame.

"Why didn't you call me? Or do you prefer just popping in and out of my life?"

"I thought you were angry at me."

"I would have forgiven you if you'd brought me to this funeral. Where did you go to after Seville?"

"Scouting for business. You know how it is—an arms salesman's work is never done."

"Liar. It's the sadistic streak in you. Come on, let's disappear before Juan finds me again."

She seemed to know her way around the Barbarossa house. We ducked behind a tapestry and then fled up a staircase to a second-floor hall.

"Are you still scouting for business—or do you have a little time to kill?"

I rubbed my hand down her back to the curve of her hip. According to the rulebook, I should have been downstairs pumping the guests, but a man has to know when to go against the rules.

"You're very dangerous for me, María."

She leaned into me and kissed my neck. "How do you mean?"

"I could be drumming up business right now."

"All work and no play...."

We tried every door in the hall until we found one that wasn't locked. Appropriately enough, it was a guest bedroom. The sheets had already been turned down.

"Hurry, Jack."

I turned the lights out. María slipped out of her dress. Her breasts were taut to the touch, their tips sweet and hard. I pushed her pants down.

"Hurry."

It was as if she thought the world was coming

to an end. Our lovemaking was hard and urgent. She opened herself to take in as much of me as possible, and then her thighs locked. My tongue probed the back of her mouth.

When I had first seen her on the beach in Ibiza, I was struck by her haughty animal leanness. In bed that haughtiness was transformed into passion. I held her straining buttocks as she pulled my lips down to her breasts. When I kissed the stiff tips, her head twisted from side to side.

At the climax her full lips drew back over a sigh of hoarse, physical satisfaction. That was the real María de Ronda. Take away the money and title, put her in bed, and the fierce female in her blossoms like a nocturnal flower. Her smile grew as we shared the orgasm, and then she locked me tight within her arms.

"That was fantastic, Jack. You were fantastic."

"Don't make it sound like the last time."

She ran her hand over the muscles of my back. "Just like a fighting bull," she whispered. "A splendid fighting bull." She kissed my lips, then raised her head. "I think somebody's going to miss us pretty soon."

We made ourselves look presentable, if not decent, and returned to the festivities. I thought our absence might not have been noticed, but Barbarossa was watching us, doing a slow burn.

"You are enjoying yourself?" he blurted out as he joined us.

"Immensely," María returned service.

"And you?" he asked me.

"As long as María's satisfied, I'm satisfied." It seemed the gallant thing to say.

"Excuse me while I go to the powder room." María exited.

Barbarossa clenched and unclenched his fists. The cocktail chatter of his guests went on.

"She is a very difficult woman," he said at last.

I resisted the temptation to contradict him. I only wanted to prod his jealousy, not set off an explosion.

"She is beautiful," I said nonchalantly. "My boss was going to put me in the London office, but I think I'll stay in Madrid now."

"Does María know this?" he asked with schoolboy fright.

"She asked me to stay."

Barbarossa lit a cigar, stalling for time to think. All his vast dreams of power hit tilt when María came into his head.

"What would convince you to leave Spain?"

He wouldn't have asked if he hadn't learned how unreliable it was to hire Gypsies to get rid of me.

"Are you talking money?" I asked casually.

He glanced around at his guests.

"That could be arranged," he whispered.

"No." I shook my head. "I have enough to suit me. The fact is that I'm just waiting for some good action to come along. I thought you might have it, but playing private guard for potash mines and real estate developments isn't my cup of tea."

That decided it for Barbarossa.

"Come with me."

He made sure that neither Vásquez nor Rojas saw us leave the ballroom. We went past the sawing violinists, through a hall hung with nudes by Rubens, and into a mahogany-panelled study. Books bound in Moroccan leather and stamped with Barbarossa's monogram filled the bookcases. There was a small bar, and beside it a globe of the world. Over the fireplace hung a coat of arms. And an immense antique desk ran almost the length of one wall. The aura was money and power, but then I'd expected that.

"Very nice."

"More than that. You asked for action. I can give you more action than you ever imagined. I told you that once before. Now I'll prove it."

His foot must have found a button on the floor. The wall behind the desk rose. In its place was an illuminated map of Spain and Morocco. Red circles marked Rota, Torrejón, and every other American base in Spain. A lone circle lay over Sidi Yahya, in the Atlas Mountains. There were also several blue circles; they pinpointed the major Spanish and Moroccan bases.

Near each circle was a jagged "SS." Barbarossa laid his finger on one of them. "Our forces. Bands of trained men ready to seize control of two countries. We call ourselves the *Sangre Sagrada,* and you can become one of us."

Sangre Sagrada. "The Sacred Blood." Just saying the words had an almost religious effect on Barbarossa. The reason for my being with him was lost in his immediate fervor.

"For seven hundred years Spain and North Africa were one people, one nation. At that time we were the most powerful country in the world. When we were divided, we each became weak. We have been weak too long.

"Now, we—the oldest families—are ready to create history again. The Sacred Blood of Spain will make our country great once more. Nothing—nobody—can stop us."

"Except Franco."

"Franco." Barbarossa scowled. "We have given up on him. I remember when he came from Africa with his Moorish troops during the war, my poor father thought that the *Caudillo* would capitalize on his success and bind the two sides of the Mediterranean together. But he can't even kick the British out of Gibraltar. So there lies Morocco with its mineral wealth and a weak king. Here lies Spain, nearly occupied by American bases, sold out by a feeble Generalísimo. One push in the right direction and it all falls into our hands. There will be power enough to share with you, Mister Finley."

I walked over to the map. The plan did have some insane logic. If it were successful, the *Sangre Sagrada*, as they called themselves, would control access to the Mediterranean. If they managed to seize the United States bases, they'd do more. In one stroke they would be a world power, at least on a par with China. Logical—but insane.

"So you have some men," I conceded. "What about money?"

Barbarossa giggled. "You know, we are not the only ones who have dreamed of uniting with North Africa."

"The French. The OSA."

"Correct. All those thousands of French officers who mutinied against De Gaulle and tried to assassinate him. They are with us, with their men and their treasury. And Germans—the Germans who have not been able to return to Germany— like Rojas. The taste for conquest is still strong in them, and they are donating their organizational experience."

"And millions in gold."

"Correct again. In return we have allowed them to incorporate the remains of the famed SS into our society. And we have given them permission to find certain professional experts."

The Werewolf would fit into that category. No wonder he'd been given that ghoulish code name.

"Why do you even need Spanish in your society if outsiders are running it?"

"This is a Spanish organization," Barbarossa exploded angrily. "The generals of the Falange have been unhappy with Franco for a long time. The *Caudillo* forsakes the ideals of the Falange to curry favor with the Opus Dei and the Vatican, with NATO and the Americans. The *Sangre Sagrada* will crawl to no one; it will take over the

American bases. The Americans will be able to do nothing, believe me."

"That's pretty unbelievable."

"How can they?" Barbarossa spread his hands. "We would have more of their planes than they would once we seized the bases. Not to mention all those nuclear weapons. Would they start a war? No, they would have to come to terms, our terms."

"A nice theory."

"This is no theory. A man has been hired. He has already struck at Franco once. An enemy agent interfered, I am told, but the agent has been disposed of." He put his fingers to his lips and laughed. "I must tell you this—you'll enjoy it. For a time we thought you might be this agent. At least I had some suspicions. You're not laughing."

"Inside I'm breaking up. But you said you failed to kill Franco."

"Failed once. That was Operation Olive Branch. Operation Eagle and Arrow will not fail. With its success we rise to lead the Spanish people. I need a good man to insure the success of our Moroccan forces. You can go to Morocco tonight and take command of a company of paratroopers. Name your price."

I took my time, memorizing the sites of his forces on the map.

"Well?" he demanded.

"Don Barbarossa, go to bed, take two aspirin, and call me in the morning if you still have a fever. This is the craziest scheme I ever heard of, and I wouldn't touch it with a ten-foot pole. Good night."

I sauntered out of the study before he could react. I was at the far end of the hall when he shouted.

"Stop! I can't let you leave now!"

He waved a gun at me threateningly. I threw open the door to the ballroom and walked out among the guests.

Barbarossa's face turned red, and he stuffed the gun into his jacket. Carrying on the conspiracy under the surface of an innocent party was one thing; shooting down a man in front of a hundred guests was another. The Werewolf would have had the cool, but not Barbarossa.

"Jack, I thought you'd disappeared from my life again," María welcomed me in the center of the ballroom.

"No, but I'm about to."

Barbarossa brushed past General Vásquez and joined us. Sweat was popping out over the fatty tissue of his neck. He hid the bulge of the gun inexpertly.

"You can't leave now," he growled.

"Sorry. Another fairy tale like that one would put me to sleep."

"What's the matter, Andrés? You seem upset."

"I asked your friend Finley to join my employment. He refused, even after I explained how much it would be to his advantage."

María lifted her dark eyebrows scornfully. "Perhaps you overestimated your charm, Andrés. Jack can do whatever he wants. Really, this is the most boring party you've ever had. I'm going home. Jack, will you escort me?"

"*Con mucho gusto.*"

As we sasheyed out of the ballroom, I looked back to see Barbarossa, Rojas, and Vásquez. The latter two were not particularly distraught, but Barbarossa was the picture of murderous impotence.

CHAPTER FIFTEEN

The body that I'd come to know so well leaned against me as we walked through the dark streets of Madrid.

"Did you two have an argument? I've never seen Andrés so upset."

"Oh, he had some idea that I told him was crazy. It's too ridiculous to even repeat."

"No, tell me."

It was late, even for Madrid. The only people remaining on the street were night watchmen and lovers.

"He thinks he's going to lead some society of nuts into power. It sounds like he's involved with the dregs of Europe—Nazis, former French colonialists, and some Spaniards who are ready to be committed. The *Sangre Sagrada*, they call themselves. A regular idiot's delight."

We passed through an archway to the large Plaza Mayor. One or two cars were parked by the central fountain, and some late diners sat at tables at the outdoor restaurants. All the shops in the arcade at the perimeter of the plaza were dark.

Next to me, I felt María stiffen.

"You have a low opinion of these conspirators," she noted.

"Should I have a high one? There's not a chance in the world of their overrunning the American bases. Oh, there would have been yesterday. Other than a wire fence, there were no safeguards to speak of then. But I sent a warning this afternoon and," I checked my wristwatch, "the troops ought to be landing just about now to reinforce the defenses."

"I thought Andrés told you about his society only tonight," María commented as we stopped by the fountain.

"He did. But I could hardly take the chance of being killed tonight and not having sent a warning. I took the chance that I was right—that Andrés was the fool, not I."

She hadn't asked me why an arms salesman would be capable of ordering troops. I didn't expect her to. I put her arm through mine and we strolled across the plaza. A few pigeons pecked at bread crumbs in the light of the gas lamps. We passed into the shadow of the arcade. The sated, after-dinner conversation of the outdoor restaurants traveled along the arcade.

"If Andrés is such a fool, how could he organize such a wide conspiracy?" María asked.

"He couldn't. It takes someone with brains, nerve, and courage. Someone from an important family, not Barbarossa's petty nobility. Someone with a taste for danger."

I stopped and lit a cigarette. The flame was reflected in her dark eyes.

"The Werewolf failed, María. You were right— I'm Killmaster. And now I know who you are. I saw the posters at the bullring. Those six bulls with the SS brand came from your ranch. They were the ones you never let me see. Then there was Andrés. Jealousy alone couldn't explain his stupidity. He wasn't just trying to impress you as a woman—you snub him too completely for that. He was trying to impress his boss. That's you— goddess and boss rolled into one."

A drunken shout came from the café at the end of the arcade. Beyond the arch in that corner of the plaza was a steep stairway down to the street that led to The Caves.

"I don't know what in the world you're talking about, Jack," she said with a sincere tone. It was too good to be true. She was offended, outraged, astonished, but she wasn't scared—and if someone accuses you of murder and you're innocent, you have to be scared.

"I mean, they never would have let me walk down Barbarossa's driveway alive if they didn't know you were going to take care of me, María. How many times is it now that you've arranged my funeral? The Gypsies, the men in the wine cellar and tonight. Is three your lucky number?"

A lattice screen ran the length of the arcade between us and the café. That was the dividing line between sunny, tourist-paradise Spain and the tortured plans of the *Sangre Sagrada*. I put my arm around María's waist and held her close to me as we walked. She tried to pull away, but I didn't let go of her. I assumed that I was in somebody's gun sights. Let him shoot around her if he wanted to.

"After all, María, I saw you kill a bull. But how defenseless you became, how helpless you were whenever you sprang an ambush. How stupid I was to fall for it for as long as I did."

"Oh, Jack, please don't say. . . ." she began as she put her arm around my neck. I grabbed her wrist and shook it. A pin fell from her fingers to the ground. A bullfighter has to know the fatal spot at the back of the neck.

"Shall we continue?" I asked and held her tighter as we walked.

Little stars of light shone through the lattice fence. The ambush must have been planned hurriedly, and her man had to be desperately waiting for her to break away from me.

"I should have let the bull kill you that day on the ranch," she smiled. All pretense was over, and she had enough class to admit it.

"That makes us even, María. There was something there between us. Who knows? In another world we might have been lovers, pure and simple.

148

But you're not pure, and I'm not simple. That's the way it goes."

I pulled out my Luger.

"There's still no way to stop us, Killmaster. I'm telling you the truth. There's no way. We will be the only ones prepared for the assassination, and we will have the government in minutes. All we need is one nuclear missile and we can destroy Gibraltar. Join us, join me. Together we can lead them."

"Not a chance. Your society is just like that corral at the bullring. As soon as the smell of blood gets in the air, you'll tear each other apart. I don't care if the lot of you go to hell and Franco has the hot-dog concession down there—I just want to keep you from dragging everyone else with you."

María stopped. She held her arms passively out of the way and tilted her face up.

"Then at least one last kiss," she asked.

That wasn't difficult. Her body melted into me the way it always did. Enemy and lover, she was both. I don't think she was false when she was passionate. But I knew she wouldn't hesitate to kill anyone in her way. Her lips were as soft as ever.

The purr of a well-tuned car filled the arcade. While María continued to kiss me, I looked over her shoulder. A glossy Mercedes limousine was gathering speed as it drove toward us. Suddenly, María pushed me away violently. The kiss had been their signal.

There was no way to reach the open space of the plaza around the lattice barrier. Between the Mercedes and the sides of the arcade there was a space of no more than two or three inches. I let go of María.

I dropped to one knee and aimed carefully. My first shot starred the windshield in front of the driver. A gunflash answered me from one foot above the windshield on the passenger's side. The car was a convertible, and the passenger was standing as he fired. At my second shot his silhouette pitched out of the car, but another man climbed into the front seat and took his place.

The car still came toward me. I aimed at the driver again, but María pulled my arm up.

"Get away!" I shouted at her.

She held onto my arm. Then the fire of a submachinegun lit up the arcade like lightning. Screams of terror poured from the café. The stone paving at my feet was shattered by lead.

María gasped and stumbled away. For one moment of pure horror I looked at her before she slumped beside a pillar. At least six bullets had ripped apart that once lovely body.

I turned and ran. The shop doorways were closed off by gates. The noise of the car grew louder. At the end of the arcade were two cafés and the long steps. The steps—and safety—were only twenty feet from my pounding shoes. I wouldn't make it.

Shop windows broke into shards of crashing glass as the submachinegun trailed after me. I fired one more desperate shot at the driver and dove headlong through a café door, landing in the sawdust at the bar.

My last shot had been a good one. The Mercedes was traveling at 60 miles an hour when it flashed by outside. It soared off the top of the stairs, over the heads of two policemen running to the shots. For thirty feet the limousine convertible was airborne.

Even where I was, on the café floor, I flinched from the heat of the crash. The Mercedes' fuel tanks ruptured as it came down on a Seat. The smaller car's fuel tanks blew, too. A column of flame reached above the roofs of the four-story buildings on both sides of the street, licking at windows and setting drapes on fire.

By the time I followed down the steps, the killers inside the Mercedes were blackened matches.

CHAPTER SIXTEEN

"The Eagle and the Arrow are the symbols of the Falange," De Lorca explained. "It must mean that the Werewolf plans to strike again when the Generalísimo addresses members of the Falange at their hall in Madrid two days from now. Only members of the Falange are allowed to attend. It could be difficult to protect Franco. General Vásquez will be at his side."

"With friends like that, who needs enemies?"

"I'm afraid you're right. Franco was once the idol of the Falange but not anymore."

We were in the communications center of Spanish Intelligence in the capital. The building housing it was of dour Victorian stone. Inside, it was computer-modern, the electronic brains taping a steady flow of coded messages from agents as far distant as Havana and Pretoria.

The colonel pointed to a glass map standing in the middle of the room.

"King Hassan has moved a division from Rabat to Sidi Yahya. We have a cruiser fifty miles off our Sahara territories to block any SS moves there. Here," he sighed with exasperation, "it's not so simple. We know about Vásquez, but how many other officers are involved? I could be sending traitors to protect our bases. It still all depends on whether we can stop the Werewolf. You don't have to worry; you've done your job."

I felt like saying that I'd heard that before. Instead I shook hands with De Lorca for what I expected was the last time and left his office.

The streets were full of *madrileños* rushing home after an honest day's work. I began to walk aimlessly. I was drained physically and emotionally. María had tried to kill me, but she'd also saved my life. She was a cold-blooded plotter but in bed she was a warm, fascinating woman. The paradoxes were getting me down.

What if the Werewolf were to succeed and the *Sangre Sagrada* did come into power? Franco had butchered his way to the top. What was I doing hanging my hide on the wall for him? It was my job to protect the security of the United States, and the security of my country included a living, breathing Franco. Granted. As Hawk would put it, nobody said I had to like it.

I ended up at the bullring, of all places. For a handful of pesetas, a guard let me in. The stands were empty. Pieces of paper swirled across the arena sand. The plaza would remain empty until Sunday and the next fights.

I still needed a vacation. My head and body ached, and I couldn't drive the names from my head, María. The Werewolf. *Sangre Sagrada.* Operation Eagle and Arrow.

A newspaper tumbled down the stands to my feet. I picked it up and read it. In a corner of the front page Franco's schedule was listed. Tomorrow the annual visit to the Valley of the Fallen, the Goliath monument to the dead of Spain's Civil War, midway between Madrid and Segovia. De Lorca had assured me that nobody would be within a hundred feet of the Generalísimo during the ceremonies. And on the day after that, his address before the Falange.

Good luck, colonel.

I balled the newspaper up and threw it down in the ring.

A night's sleep made a difference. As my eyes opened, I reached for the phone. It took Spanish Intelligence all of ten seconds to locate De Lorca.

"The assassination attempt," I said, "it won't be at the Falange Hall. It will be made today."

"What makes you think that?"

"Have a car here in ten minutes and I'll tell you on the way. And bring some coffee."

De Lorca was outside the hotel in exactly nine minutes. *"Buenos días,"* he offered as he opened the door for me.

154

"*Buenos días,* yourself. When do the ceremonies start at the Valley of the Fallen?"

"In three hours. With our siren we will be there in one."

His driver was already piercing the traffic on the Avenida Generalísimo. Seats and motorcycles got out of our way.

"Now, why are we rushing? What is this idea of yours?"

"Not my idea, it's the Werewolf's. Look, if the Werewolf were to strike tomorrow at the Hall, what would you say his odds would be on escaping with his life?"

"Hmm, not terribly good. There would be a considerable panic, but you know Franco's bodyguards. The Werewolf would have to be close, since the podium will be crowded. Franco could move, and the assassin might hit Vásquez instead. A shot from within twenty or thirty feet."

"Good odds for a fanatic but bad for a professional who wants to live."

"But the name of the operation, 'Eagle and Arrow.' It refers to the Falange."

The powerful car shot up the boulevard. We passed the Air Ministry on the left.

"I don't think so. The name of the operation has bugged me all night. I woke up with the answer. Remember the name of the other operation. Olive Branch. The name described the technique of the assassination attempt, not the setting. Did the Werewolf strike at a peace conference? No," I answered my own question. "The Olive Branch was the package the bird was carrying to Franco. The bird was a dove of peace, a peace over Franco's dead body."

"And how do you interpret 'Eagle and Arrow'?"

"It's simple once you put yourself in the Werewolf's place and keep in mind that escape is as important as success. Kill and get away. The Arrow is him. The Eagle is his escape—a plane or a helicopter. Now you can't put a plane or a helicopter down in the Falange Hall, but you sure can in a valley."

De Lorca slouched with thought. Finally he tapped the driver's shoulder. "Hurry, Guillermo."

The Valley of the Fallen is an impressive memorial for any war. Next to a flat plain is a saddle-backed mountain that has been turned into a common grave for thousands of unknown Spanish soldiers who fell on both sides of the Civil War. Veterans who had arrived by early trains and buses wandered around greeting old comrades.

De Lorca and I pushed our way through them and climbed a tremendous outdoor stairway to a vast terrace, constructed of black marble. It was here, seemingly out of reach of any danger, that Franco would read his speech.

"I don't know, Nick. Even with a telescopic sight, he has to be within three thousand yards for a kill shot. Look at this crowd of veterans. They'll fill the valley for a mile back. The Werewolf wouldn't need a plane to escape—he'd need a miracle."

The colonel had a point. In the usual mass of

civilians the Werewolf might expect some confusion after he fired. These veterans would know a rifle shot when they heard it.

What if the Werewolf used a larger-caliber weapon, perhaps a rocket released from the far side of the valley? The only other person on the platform during the ceremony would be the cardinal of Madrid. To murder him along with Franco would certainly destroy any claims to respectability that the *Sangre Sagrada* might have.

It had to be a relatively small-caliber weapon, one to be fired three times at the most. But from where? Nowhere.

Behind us was a stupefyingly great mass of the same black marble as the terrace.

"What's this?"

"Didn't you know? I thought you appreciated the irony," De Lorca grinned. "It's Franco's burial vault. He built it for himself. A modest tomb for a modest man. Even a humble marker, don't you think?"

The Intelligence Officer was sardonically referring to the enormous black cross that rose a thousand feet in the air at the front of the valley. I had first seen it when we were approaching the valley.

"Let's just make sure the tomb doesn't claim Franco before he's prepared," I suggested.

We entered the mausoleum. It had the hushed, claustrophobic atmosphere of a grave, and chapels with votive candles lined a low-ceilinged hall. The sound of the crowd was suddenly far behind us, and our footsteps reverberated along the ebony marble.

If you were a lover of black marble busts of Francisco Franco, this was the place to spend a full day. I had to admit I was glad to leave the tomb, with or without the Werewolf.

"No megalomania there," I remarked as De Lorca and I emerged.

"No assassin either, *amigo*. I think you can take your hunch back to bed."

"Sorry."

"*De nada*. You might as well remain for the ceremony now. I'll drive you back to Madrid afterwards."

"Sure."

De Lorca had to stay by the platform to oversee the rest of the security arrangements. I wandered back to his car to watch the show.

A sea of veterans filled the valley floor. Many were in their old uniforms, and the smell of mothballs competed with the fragrance of the wine sacks that were being passed back and forth. On the platform a podium and a microphone were installed. The legionnaires arrived and made the same inspection of the mausoleum we had. Franco's arrival was imminent—you could feel the tension in the crowd.

Dictator or not, this was the man who had symbolized their country for three generations. This was a monument not just to himself but to all who had fallen in a savage war. Excitement

ran through the crowd as the word traveled that
Franco and the cardinal were approaching.

Guillermo, the colonel's driver, aimed his camera
at the platform, twisting the lens back and forth
with frustration. "I borrowed this camera just so
I could get a good picture. Now it doesn't work.
I can't get it to focus."

The camera was a handsome Nikon 35 mm
equipped with a long-focus lens. I trained it on
the platform and quickly brought the podium into
focus.

"It works," I said. "You were trying to focus
with the ring that controls the lens aperture."

Franco's head seemed startlingly close as he
climbed the steps to the platform.

"Oh, quick, give it to me," the driver pleaded.

"Just a second."

I swung the camera around to catch the mass of
soldiers. Then I followed along the line of official
cars. And around to the cross. I followed the long
stem of it to the top and my fingers froze.

There on the top of the cross was a glimmer of
metal that would have been invisible to the un-
aided eye. There, too, was the one place an assassin could sit in comfort and pick his shot, undis-
turbed by the crowd. When the shot struck home,
no one could touch him, because somewhere, already aloft, a helicopter with a rope ladder waited
to lift the Werewolf from the cross.

I checked the range on the side of the lens—
eighteen hundred yards. An easy shot for a professional. There wasn't enough time for me to

reach the platform. Also, if the Werewolf saw me, he would be sure to fire on Franco at once.

"*Soldados y cristianos, estamos aquí por. . . .*" the cardinal's voice boomed through the loud-speakers. Franco was on the Cardinal's right. As soon as the prelate stepped back, the assassin would have a clear shot.

I walked at a fast pace toward the base of the cross. Picture the Washington Monument. Make it black and give it the short arms of a cross, and you'll understand how this cross towered over the assembly. And why the caretaker at the base refused to let me in.

"The elevator is locked. It is always locked during the leader's speches. No one is allowed up."

"Someone is up there right now."

"Impossible. The elevator has been off all day."

"Then he came last night. I haven't got time to argue."

He was a righteous old man in a rusty suit that must have been twenty years old. A single medal was pinned to his lapel. "Leave," he ordered. "Another word and I will call the Guardia Civil. Nobody dares make trouble when the *Caudillo* is here."

I hated to do it. I yanked his sleeve and as he stumbled forward, slapped my thumb and finger on the pressure points of his neck. He passed out standing up. I apologized and sat him down in his chair.

I entered the base of the cross. It was about thirty by forty feet here and tapered to five by

160

seven feet at the top. The elevator rose only as far as the arms of the cross. And the elevator was locked.

". . . *porque la historia de un país es más que memoria.* . . ." the cardinal droned on, but for how much longer?

I used the caretaker's key to open the elevator's lock. As soon as the padlock was off, I jumped into the small car and pushed the button for *ARRIBA*. The elevator's motor came to life, and with a click the car started up.

The Werewolf would hear the elevator. No doubt he could even feel it vibrate as he lay on top of the cross. It might hurry his shot, but on the other hand, he was a professional. He wouldn't panic. He would probably figure it was police in the elevator, but he had no reason to believe they suspected he was there. He could afford to ignore their visit, I hoped.

The elevator seemed to take forever. Through occasional gunslit windows I could mark the changes in altitude, but I couldn't tell whether the cardinal's speech had ended and Franco's had begun.

The car reached the small observation area at the arms of the cross. I stepped out and heard with relief that the cardinal was still orating, but his speech was coming to a close.

There was a chair for people who grew faint during ascents in the cross. I pulled it under a panel in the platform's low ceiling. On my third try I found the caretaker's key that fit, and the panel swung open.

"... *Ahora, con la gracia de Dios y la destina de España, El Caudillo.*"

The Cardinal would be taking his step back, and Franco would be putting his short arms around the podium and facing his old comrades in arms. The effect as the bullet hit would be stunning.

I pulled myself up through the panel. The area was no more than a clear space, a hollow with no light. My hands felt over the walls and found rungs.

The Werewolf would aim for the ear. There is a radius of two inches from the eardrum that is fatal. The telescopic sight would zero in, the crossbars centering between tragus and lobe.

At the top of the rungs was an overhead panel. Light leaked out around its edges. I heard the shallow intake of breath that precedes the squeeze of the trigger.

I slammed the panel up with my gun. Two thousand yards away a 7.62 mm slug with a solid head brushed the back of Franco's head and scarred the marble terrace. He looked up, breaking off his speech, and saw the score mark. The legionnaires rushed up the stairs to form a protective cordon around him. The crowd was in pandemonium.

My hand was caught in the panel. The Werewolf's foot was on it, pushing the metal edge into my wrist. I swung to the side. Two slugs punched down at me through the center of the panel, whistling past my chest. As he paused, I hit the panel with my free hand, shoving it and him up.

The Werewolf staggered back to the edge of a small square of marble. Beyond that loomed a thousand feet of air. But somehow he transferred his weight to the balls of his feet and didn't fall. By now I'd crawled up to the top and joined him, my Luger pointed at the buckle of his belt. His rifle was aimed at my heart.

"Back from the dead, Killmaster. You are a tough one to put away. I should have simply put a bullet in you before."

The rifle was weightless in his arms. How could I ever have taken this man for an old peasant? He was dressed like a company president on vacation —blazer and ascot, tailored slacks and expensive Wellington boots. A little gray tinged his dark hair, and his eyes were the color of metal traps. He reminded me of myself. It was an eerie sensation.

"Too late, Werewolf. Or do you want to tell me your real name?"

"Go to hell."

"It looks as if one of us has an appointment there. I think it's you. That's a sport-model rifle, and it carries only three cartridges at a time. You've used them. You've struck out."

Down on the platform the legionnaires had discovered the source of the shot. All they could tell was that there were two figures on top of the cross. A jeep with a mounted machinegun rolled up to the base, its gun tracking up the marble stem to us.

I dove as the bullets swept past. The Werewolf gripped his rifle like a club and brought it down on my gun. A second swing caught me in the chest, knocking me to the edge.

The polished marble was slippery under my knees. I couldn't get close to the Werewolf because I was ducking the stock of his rifle and he was forcing me back. The stock dug into my ribs, then my stomach. I folded my arms over my head.

He kept glancing over my shoulder, and suddenly I heard the rotors of a helicopter. Eagle was picking up Arrow according to plan. The wash of the blades tugged at us. Between my arms I saw the dancing length of a rope ladder.

"You lose, Killmaster."

The Werewolf pounded the rifle on my forearms once more before grasping the ladder. The helicopter began to pull away and his feet left the top of the cross.

I pushed myself off my knees and leaped into the air, wrapping my arms around his legs. The rope swung wildly with our double weight, causing the pilot to panic and lift us too fast.

The rope broke. I let go of the Werewolf and fell, landing some twenty feet below, spread-eagled on the bar of the cross. My ears were ringing, and my chest felt permanently flattened but I dragged myself to the edge and looked down.

The Werewolf was still falling. The crowd at the base of the cross dispersed. He hit, and there was nothing left of the Werewolf but his code name.

CHAPTER SEVENTEEN

The warm sun of Ibiza tanned my outside while a rum punch cooled my inside. I lay back on the beach chair and relaxed.

The Werewolf and María were dead. Barbarossa changed his residence to Switzerland. Vásquez put a gun to his own head and pulled the trigger. The *Sangre Sagrada* burst like a balloon.

Now Hawk swore on a stack of confidential reports that I really was going to have my vacation. No more interruptions unless it was the end of the world. Well, you have to trust him sometime.

A beach ball bounced on the sand and landed on my sunglasses. Reflexively I caught both my glasses and the ball.

"Could I have my ball back, please."

I sat up.

The owner of this particular ball was in a white

bikini. Rather, little triangles of white bathing suit were not covering very much of a fantastic female figure. She had long black hair and wide-apart dark eyes. I felt that I'd been through this scene before.

"This looks like a valuable beach ball. Can you prove it's yours?"

"It doesn't have my name on it, if that's what you mean," she said.

"That is a problem. First tell me if you are Spanish."

"No," she smiled. "I'm American."

"And you're not a countess?"

She shook her head. The top of the bikini jiggled enticingly, but I had to be careful this time around.

"And you don't breed bulls, and you have nothing to do with plots to overthrow any government?"

"None of those. I'm a dental technician from Chicago, and I just want my beach ball."

"Ah," I sighed with satisfaction and pulled another chair close to mine. "Now we can proceed to the name stage. I'm Jack Finley."

As she sat down, I signaled the bar for another round of drinks.

Nick Carter in an unbeatable spy adventure series

Science Fiction in Tandem editions

Planet of No Return Poul Anderson 25p
    Man must search for colonies beyond the stars, but
    can he find a permanent home there?

The Time-Hoppers Robert Silverberg 25p
    Every human need was fulfilled in the 25th century,
    yet they still yearned to escape

Hawksbill Station Robert Silverberg 25p
    Banished from the complicated world of the far
    future to the barren emptiness of the remote past

The Man in the Maze Robert Silverberg 25p
    Solitary and embittered, hiding from the loathing of
    his fellows, he must be lured out of his refuge to save
    the world

Light a Last Candle Vincent King 25p
    'Vivid stuff, a tale of internecine strife between
    mutated and modified people in the far future.'
    Edmund Cooper, Sunday Times

Farewell, Earth's Bliss D. G. Compton 25p
    Their past was Earth, their present a colony on Mars
    —and their future?

The Time Mercenaries Philip E. High 25p
    They were a thousand years out of date, and the
    planet's only chance to defeat the alien invaders

Donovan's Brain Curt Siodmak 25p
    Doomed by disease, mangled in a plane crash, there
    was no doubt that Donovan was dead. Yet his brain
    lived!

Vornan 19 Robert Silverberg 30p
    He appeared suddenly and mysteriously, claiming
    to be a visitor from the year 2999. But his evidence
    was not totally convincing

Let The Spacemen Beware Poul Anderson 25p
    Why did the gentle people of Gwydonia become like
    savages at Bale-time? And was their strange be-
    haviour connected with the red flower that bloomed
    everywhere on the planet?

Fantasy Fiction in Tandem editions

By John Jakes

A warrior's sword against the sorcery of ancient evil

Brak the Barbarian ..	..	..	..	..	..	25p
Brak the Barbarian—The Sorceress		..	..	..		25p
Brak the Barbarian—The Mark of the Demons ..				..		25p

By Andre Norton

'Rich, brilliant, superbly imaginative and fully adult pure fantasy' *Lin Carter*

Witch World..	..	..	..	..	..	25p
Web of the Witch World	..	..	..	..	..	25p
Three Against the Witch World	..	..	..	..		25p
Warlock of the Witch World		..	..	..	..	25p
Sorceress of the Witch World		..	..	..	..	25p
Year of the Unicorn	..	..	..	..	..	25p

By Ursula LeGuin

Hugo and Nebula Award winning writer

Planet of Exile	..	..	..	..	..	25p
Rocannon's World	..	..	..	..	..	25p

By John Norman

The Chronicles of Counter-Earth

Outlaw of Gor	..	..	..	..	..	35p
Priest-Kings of Gor		..	..	..	..	40p
Nomads of Gor	..	..	..	..	..	40p
Assassin of Gor	..	..	..	..	..	40p
Tarnsman of Gor	..	..	..	..	..	30p

Non-fiction in Tandem editions

Occult and the Unusual in Tandem editions

Horror in Tandem editions

The Way of An Eagle   Dan Potter   30p

He came on a gleaming white motorcycle and some people said that he looked like an eagle descending from the sky. Was he a turned-on no-good looking for trouble, a reincarnated James Dean, or was he a messenger of peace and goodwill? To some he was beauty and kindness, but to the town hoodlums he was something they didn't understand, instinctively feared, and had to destroy.

The Plasticine Man   Erika Maharg   25p

Bull Harrigan was many things to many people. A man for all seasons, all reasons, every-woman's personal lover. He had come to Spain to enjoy himself and he had neither the will-power not the inclination to refuse the women who needed and wanted him. But they always demanded more than he was prepared to give, sometimes more than he felt he had. He wished they would stop trying to mould him into what they wanted him to be.

Where's Poppa?   Robert Klane   25p

Some people have all the luck. Money and jobs and girls. Especially girls. Gordon Hocheiser had the job, and the money, but whenever he thought he was getting anywhere near a girl, there was Momma. Momma – sitting in the apartment, waiting for Poppa to come home, and seeing to it that no one but herself laid hands on her son. Momma was quite a woman!

Four great Westerns
by the Spur Award Winning Writer

Louis L'Amour

Kilkenny

Lance Kilkenny was one of the fastest guns in the West, a man who could follow a trail better than an Apache. Now he wanted peace and was prepared to fight for it, to kill or be killed.

Crossfire Trail

Rafe Caredec would never have gone to Crazy Woman Canyon if it hadn't been for a promise. What he didn't know was that he was sitting on a hidden fortune that attracted lawlessness, murder and trigger-passion from every corner of the Territory.

Utah Blaine

Red Creek was a town where the law went masked and unmasked, and both kinds were out to finish Blaine before he put paid to the land-grabber. There was just one thing they hadn't reckoned on: Utah Blaine was as big as the legends made him.

Showdown at Yellow Butte

When Tom Kedrick found himself at the head of a gang of hired killers, it took a no-quarter battle between the settlers and the bush-whackers to show Kedrick the truth. Then he knew there was only one way for him to stop the blood bath he had started.

Tandem edition 25p

Stephen John

I Like It That Way

Follow the outrageous adventures of offbeat art dealer Albert Divine. Aided and abetted throughout by his voluptuous model girl friend, Angela, he succumbs to much skulduggery in the spheres of art and bed during a meteoric rise which hurtles him into the orgiastic orbits of some pretty peculiar characters. Not for the squeamish, the humourless or the intolerant, it makes the Permissive Society seem like a Victorian vicarage tea party.

How About This Way?

Art dealer extraordinary, Albert Divine, is on the rampage again. This time, in the freaky world of the weird and beautiful people on the Riviera, he is overcome in turn by the sun, the liquor, and a variety of lustful ladies. His host's totally original hobby of re-enacting scenes from great paintings, embellished by what the artist dared not paint, involves Albert with an enthusiastic group of tourists who finally let down their bikinis for a re-staging of that masterpiece, the *Rape of the Sabines*.

Any Way You Like

An all-expenses-paid trip in search of ithy-phallic statuettes and virility fetishes takes Albert to Africa. There he rubs more than shoulders with the accomplished explorer Gloria Eisenway whose book *Getting It Up In Africa* involves some amazing research. Angela, too, finds the climate stimulating, and discovers a new outlet for her talents playing a leading role in a tribal fertility rite.

and

This Way, Please!

'How Albert manages to keep it up I shall never know.'
Ariadne, Amanda, Angela, Jane, Lavinia, Alison. . . .

Name ....

Address ....

Titles required ....

....

....

....

....

....

....

....

- - - - - - - - - - - - - - - - - - -

The publishers hope that you enjoyed this book and invite you to write for the full list of Tandem titles.

If you find any difficulty in obtaining these books from your usual retailer we shall be pleased to supply the titles of your choice – packing and postage 5p per book – upon receipt of your remittance.

WRITE NOW TO:
Universal-Tandem Publishing Co. Ltd.,
14 Gloucester Road,
London SW7 4RD